Raves For the Work of
LAWRENCE BLOCK!

"There is only one writer of mystery and detective fiction who comes close to replacing the irreplaceable John D. MacDonald…The writer is Lawrence Block."
—*Stephen King*

"Block grabs you…and never lets go."
—*Elmore Leonard*

"Brilliant…For clean, close-to-the-bone prose, the line goes from Dashiell Hammett to James M. Cain to Lawrence Block. He's that good."
—*Martin Cruz Smith*

"The suspense mounts & mounts & mounts…very superior."
—*James M. Cain*

"A master of crime fiction."
—*Jonathan Kellerman*

"The reader is riveted to the words, the action."
—*Robert Ludlum*

"Lawrence Block is addictive. Make room on your bookshelf."
—*David Morrell*

She'd changed her clothes for dinner. Now she wore a very simple black dress with a scoop neckline. A green heart hung from a small gold chain around her throat, a very deep green against her white skin. Jade, I guessed.

I ran through it for her and she nodded, taking it all in. Usually I hate having an amateur in on things too deeply, but she seemed to have a feeling for the game. It wasn't necessary to tell her things twice. She listened very intently with those brown eyes opened very wide and she hung on every word.

A busboy cleared our table. We passed up dessert and had coffee and cognac. The cognac was very old and very smooth. I broke out a fresh pack of cigarettes. She took one. I gave her a light and she leaned forward to take it. The jade heart fell away from her white skin. The black dress fell forward, too, and there was a momentary flash of the body beneath it, the thrust of breasts.

Our eyes locked and we smiled foolishly at each other.

She was very damned good for an amateur. She had the brains for it, and the right attitude. She was a natural girl for the grift. If this fell in, I thought, or even if it didn't, she could probably make a damned fine living as the female half of a badger game combo. She sure as hell had the looks for it.

She said, "You know, I was very nervous about all of this before tonight, John. I'm not nervous any more."

"What changed your mind?"

"You did..."

The GIRL with the LONG GREEN HEART

by Lawrence Block

A HARD CASE CRIME NOVEL

A HARD CASE CRIME BOOK

(HCC-014)

November 2005

Published by

Dorchester Publishing Co., Inc.
200 Madison Avenue
New York, NY 10016

in collaboration with Winterfall LLC

*This book is a work of fiction. Names, characters, places, and
incidents either are the products of the author's imagination or
are used fictitiously, and any resemblance to actual events or
persons, living or dead, is entirely coincidental.*

ISBN 0-8439-5585-6

The name "Hard Case Crime" and the Hard Case Crime logo
are trademarks of Winterfall LLC. Hard Case Crime books are
selected and edited by Charles Ardai.

Printed in the United States of America

Visit us on the web at *www.HardCaseCrime.com*

for BETSY and PO

THE GIRL WITH THE LONG GREEN HEART

One

When the phone rang I was shaving. I put my razor down and walked across the room to pick up the phone on the bedside table.

A woman's voice said, "It's eight-thirty, Mr. Hayden."

I thanked her and went back to finish shaving. I put on a plain white shirt and the good blue suit I had bought in Toronto. I picked out a dark blue tie with an unobtrusive below-the-knot design and tied it three times before I got the knot as small as I wanted it. I gave my shoes a brief rubdown with one of the hotel's hand towels, got the day's first cigarette going, and went over to my window to have a look at the city.

It was my first real look at Olean. I had gotten into town the night before on a puddle-jump flight from Toronto to Buffalo to Olean. My cab ride in from the airport had been less than a scenic tour. At that hour the city looked like any small town with everything closed. There were two movie houses, the Olean and the Palace, and one had already turned off its marquee. A few bars were open. I had gone straight to the Olean House and straight to bed.

Now, in daylight, the town still had little to set it

apart. My room was on the third of four floors, and my window looked out across North Union Street. The Olean Trust Company was directly across the street, flanked by a chain five-and-dime and a small drugstore. The street ran to eight lanes, with cars parked at angles to the curb on both sides of the street. Most of the parking spaces were taken.

On the extreme right, I could just see the Exchange National Bank building. It was eight stories tall, twice as high as any of the buildings near it. Wallace J. Gunderman had an office in it, on the sixth floor.

I went downstairs. There were no messages for me. The gray-haired woman at the desk asked me if I would be staying another night. I said that I would. I picked up the local paper at the newsstand in the lobby and carried it into the hotel coffee shop. Businessmen and secretaries sat around drinking morning coffee. I took a table in front, near a group of lawyers who were discussing a hearing on a zoning ordinance. I ate scrambled eggs and bacon and drank black coffee and read everything of interest in the Olean *Times-Herald*. Gunderman's name kept cropping up. He was on a committee of the City Club, he was heading up the Men's Division of the United Fund campaign—that sort of thing.

I had a second cup of coffee and signed the check. Outside, the air was warm and clear. I walked the length of the block, turned and came back to the hotel. It was nine-thirty when I got back to my room. I looked up Gunderman's number in the phone book and gave it to the hotel operator.

A girl said, "Mr. Gunderman's office, good morning."

"Mr. Gunderman, please."

"May I ask who's calling?"

"John Hayden. I represent the Barnstable Corporation."

There was a very brief pause, a short intake of breath. "One moment, please," she said. "I'll see if Mr. Gunderman is in."

I lit a cigarette while she saw if Mr. Gunderman was in. When he came on the line he sounded younger than I had pictured him. His voice was deep and resonant.

"Mr. Hayden? Wallace Gunderman. I don't believe I know you, do I?"

"No," I said. "I'm representing the Barnstable Corporation, Mr. Gunderman, and I wondered if I could drop by and see you sometime this afternoon."

"You're here in Olean?"

"That's right."

"Could you tell me what you want to see me about?"

"Of course. It's our understanding, sir, that you own a fairly sizable tract of land in northern Alberta. Our corporation is a Toronto-based outfit interested in—"

"Oh, so that's it."

"Mr. Gunderman—"

"Now you wait a minute, sir." He was a few decibels

short of a full-fledged roar. "You must think I'm an awfully stupid man, Mr. Hayden. You must think that just because a man's been played for a sucker once he can be raked over the same coals forever. I took a neat beating on that Canadian land. I made the mistake of listening to one of you smooth-talking Canuck salesmen and I fell for his line like a ton of bricks. I shelled out one hell of a lot of money for some of the most useless land in the world."

I let him go on. He was doing nicely.

"That was five years ago, Hayden. It took me a while to quit being ashamed of myself. I'm not ashamed any more. I was a damn fool. I've been a damn fool before, and I'll probably be one again before I die, but I've never been enough of a damn fool to make the same mistake twice. You people took me once. You taught me a lesson, and goddamn it, I learned that lesson. I'm not in the market for another patch of moose pasture, thank you."

"Mr. Gunderman—"

"For Christ's sake, don't you get the message? I'm not interested."

"Just let me say one thing, Mr. Gunderman."

"You're just wasting your time. And my time as well."

"There's just one point of misunderstanding, Mr. Gunderman, and as soon as we clear the air on that I think you'll see my point."

"I already see your point."

I took a breath. I said, "Mr. Gunderman, you seem

to think that I'm interested in selling you land at inflated prices. That's not my intention. I'm here in Olean to make a firm offer on behalf of the Barnstable Corporation to *buy* your land *from* you."

There was a fairly long pause. I put my cigarette out in the ashtray.

"Did I hear you right, Mr. Hayden?"

"I said I'm here to make you an offer for your land in Alberta," I said. "We wrote to you not long ago but never received an answer."

"I never got that letter."

"I'm sure it was sent. In any case—"

"Just a minute. Maybe my girl can dig up that letter. That's the Barnstable Corporation?"

"Yes."

I held on while he sent his secretary on a search of the files. I had a fresh cigarette working by the time he was back on the line. His voice was pitched a lot lower now. He sounded almost apologetic.

"I have that letter after all," he said. "It's from someone named Rance."

"Douglas Rance. That's our company president."

"And you are—"

"Just a hired hand, Mr. Gunderman."

"I see." He thought that over. "According to this letter, you people want to purchase my Canadian holdings for a combination preserve and hunting lodge. Is that right?"

"That's right."

"Well, I can't understand how I overlooked this

letter, Mr. Hayden. I must have thought it was a solici-
tation of one sort or another and just tossed it aside,
and then it wound up in the files. I'm sorry for the attitude I took before."

"Oh, I can understand that."

"You could if you'd ever been taken by those
swindlers. No reflection on your country, Mr. Hayden,
but there are a lot of smooth operators based on your
side of the border. You say you want my land for a
hunting lodge?"

"Yes, that's right."

"Well, I'd like to give this some thought before I
see you. You said you're here in town. Where can
I reach you?"

"I'm at the Olean House. Room 309."

"You'll be there for the next hour or so?"

"Yes."

"Then I'll call you within the hour."

He called at ten. I picked up the phone on the third
ring. This time around he was slicker than oil. Was I
free for lunch? I said I was. Could I drop over to his
office around noon? I could. He was at the Exchange
Bank building, and did I know where that was? I did.
Well, good. He would see me then.

I got to his office a few minutes after twelve. His name
was listed on the building directory downstairs, just his
name and the number of his office. I rode an out-
moded elevator to the sixth floor and found my way
around the corridors to a door with his name on it. It

opened into an anteroom. There were bookshelves and a magazine rack to the left. On the right side was a steel desk with a girl behind it.

Quite a girl. Her hair was a deep chestnut brown and there was a lot of it. Her eyes were large, and just a shade lighter than her hair. She looked up from her typewriter and gave me a smile filled with sugar and spice and everything nice. Could she help me?

"I'm John Hayden," I said. "I've an appointment with Mr. Gunderman."

The eyes brightened and the smile spread. She looked as though she wanted to say something. Her tongue flicked over her lips and she got to her feet.

"Just one moment," she said. "I'll tell Mr. Gunderman that you're here."

She walked through a door marked *Wallace Gunderman Private*. I watched her go. She was worth watching. She was a tall girl, almost my height, and she had a shape to carry the height. Slender enough to be called willowy, but a little too full in bust and hips for that tag. She wore a skirt and sweater. Both were probably too tight. I wasn't about to complain.

The door closed after her. When it opened a second time she led Wallace J. Gunderman out of it. She stepped aside and he came across the room to shake my hand.

"Mr. Hayden? I'm Wally Gunderman. Hope I didn't keep you waiting."

"Not at all."

"Good," he said. He was a tall, thick-set man with

iron-gray hair and bushy eyebrows and a sunlamp tan. He could have posed for Calvert ads. "Have you met my secretary, Mr. Hayden? Mr. Hayden, this is Evelyn Stone. Evvie's the girl who managed to bury your Mr. Rance's letter in the files."

"I was *sure* you'd seen that letter, Mr. Gunderman—"

"And maybe I did, dear. At least you didn't throw it away." He laughed. "But we can forget that now. I'm just glad you people didn't let the matter drop after one letter. Do you like Italian food, Mr. Hayden? Because there's a pretty good Italian place around the block."

"Sounds fine to me."

"Good," he said.

His car was parked in front of the building in a spot reserved for him. It was a Lincoln Continental, a convertible, dove-gray with lighter gray leather upholstery. He had the top down.

"Beautiful weather these past few weeks," he said. "We usually get a lot of rain in September, but so far it's held off. How's the weather in Toronto?"

"Cooler than this, but nice."

"And I suppose the winters are equally bad here and there. You have it colder, but we get a little more in the way of snow. You don't have a Canadian accent. Are you originally from Canada?"

"Not even close. I was born in New Mexico, near the Colorado border."

"Been in Canada long?"

"Not very long."

We made exciting talk like that while he drove the few blocks to the restaurant. It was called Piccioli's. There was a small bar, and the tables were covered with red checkered cloths.

"Not fancy," Gunderman said, "but clean, and the food's good."

They had a fairly good crowd for lunch. Gunderman had a booth reserved and we went to it. A slim dark-eyed waitress brought us drinks, Scotch with water for him and a martini for me. Gunderman said the Italian specialties were very good, but that I could get a decent steak if I wanted one. I ordered lasagna. He had one of the veal dishes with spaghetti.

The lunch conversation was small talk that avoided the main issue very purposefully. I followed his lead. We talked about Canada, about his one trip to the American Far West. He asked me if I'd been to Olean before, and I said I hadn't.

"It's not a bad little town," he said. "A good place to live. We're a little off the beaten track here. Up along the Mohawk Valley, the Erie Canal route, it's one town after another. You've got a lot of growth there but you've got all the problems of that kind of growth, the slums, everything. We don't have that kind of growth but at the same time we're not stagnant, not by a long shot. And there are a few stagnant areas in this state, John. I don't know if you've ever been in the central part of New York State, but you take a county like Schoharie County, for example—why, they've got less population today than they did during the Civil War. We've had steady growth, not tremendous growth but just healthy growth."

We were John and Wally now. He added cream to his coffee and settled back in his chair.

"I certainly can't complain," he said. "This town has been good to me."

"You've lived here all your life?"

"All my life. Oil made this town, you know. You could figure that from the name of the city. Olean, like oleaginous or oleomargarine. Oil. The oil fields here and in northern Pennsylvania were producing around the time that Oklahoma was just a place to dump Indians. And the wells still pump oil. Secondary and tertiary extractions, and not as important as they were once, but that oil still comes up."

"Is that where you got started?"

"That's where the money first came from." He grinned. "My father was a wildcat driller, bought up oil leases and sank holes in the ground. He was in the right spot at the right time and he made his pile and it was a good-sized pile, believe me. I still see income from wells that he drilled."

"I see."

"But I never did much with oil myself. My dad died, oh, it's about thirty years now. I wasn't thirty myself then and there I was, his sole heir, with a guaranteed income from the wells and a pretty large amount of principal, and this with the country right in the middle of the Depression. Everybody figured me to move to

New York or some place like that and just live on income. I surprised them. Know what I did?"

"What?"

"I started buying land like a crazy man. Scrap land and wasteland and farm land that wasn't paying its way and timber land with the hardwood growth all cut and gone. Land nobody wanted, and this was in the thirties when land was so cheap you could have had an option on the whole state of Nebraska for maybe a dollar and fifty cents. That's an exaggeration, but you know what I mean. Land was cheap, and the craziest damned fool in creation was the man interested in buying it. At least that was what people thought. Hell, there would be a piece of land where the oil rights had already been sold, and where there was no oil there anyway, nothing but rocky soil, and I would go and buy it, and you can't blame the people for thinking I was out of my mind."

"But I guess you made out all right, Wally."

He laughed like a volcano erupting. He was enjoying himself now. "Well, I guess they found out who was crazy," he said. "One thing about land, there's only so much of it in the world, and there won't ever be more. Every year there's more people in this country, and every year there's more industry and more housing and more of everything else, and there's always the same amount of land. And the best thing to buy for the long pull is the land nobody wants. You buy it and hang onto it and sooner or later somebody wants it, and then he has to pay your price for it. When they were looking to put up a shopping plaza east of the city, it was my land they picked for it. When they decided to cut Route 17 as a four-lane divided highway from Jamestown to New York, I was sitting with the land on either side of the old two-lane road. And when some smart boys figured out the money they could make growing Christmas trees on scrub land, and they wanted to buy in this area, I had a hell of a lot of land for them to pick from that I'd bought awful damned cheap. So you can say I made out all right, John. There's some chunks of land around here that I bought twenty years ago and couldn't get my money out of today, but there aren't many like that. And I'm happy to keep them anyway. They'll pay off, sooner or later."

I made the appropriate comment and started on my coffee. He lit up a cigar and chewed the end of it for a few minutes.

Then he said, "That's what burned me the most about that tract of moose pasture up in Canada. Here those sharpshooters took me at my own game. Here I am in the land business, buying land cheap all over the Southern Tier, and they sell me useless land at such a high price I still can't believe I went for it. You know about that promotion?"

"Just how much land you hold, and that you're supposed to have paid a pretty stiff price for it."

"Stiff." He finished his coffee. "You don't know the half of it. I got a fast-talking sharpie who called me on the phone and went on about uranium strikes in the area and how his real estate brokerage house wanted to turn over a lot of land in a hurry, and how the uranium rights were sure to sell on a terrific royalty arrangement, and he sent along just enough in the way of promotional material to make me convinced I was getting in on the ground floor of the greatest bargain since the Dutch bought Manhattan Island. I went for it like a fish for a worm. Except it wasn't even a worm on that hook, it was a lure, and when I bit on it I was hooked through the gills and back out again. All that money for some acreage I could graze reindeer on, if I had some reindeer."

"Didn't you have any legal recourse?"

"Not a bit. That was the hell of it. Everything they did was legal. They were contracting to sell me land, and they sold it, and I bought it, and it was mine and my money was theirs and that was that. I don't think they could have pulled it off in the States. But Canada's a little more lenient when it comes to government regulation. They get away with murder up there."

He shook his head. "But I'm running off at the mouth. Anyway, I guess we're back to the subject that got us here in the first place. We're talking about my stretch of land. You want to buy it, is that right?"

"That's right."

"Well, I won't say it's not for sale. What kind of an opening offer did you have in mind?"

"I believe there was a figure mentioned in Mr. Rance's letter," I said carefully.

"There was, yes, but I thought it was just a feeler. There was an offer of five hundred dollars."

"Well that's what I'm prepared to offer, Wally."

He grinned. "As an opening offer?"

"As a firm price."

The grin faded. "That's a hell of a figure," he said. "If you had any idea what that hunk of property cost me—"

"Yes, but of course you paid an inflated price for it."

"Still and all, I sank all of twenty thousand dollars into that land. There's an even seventy-five hundred acres of it, most of it in Alberta but a little chunk edging into Saskatchewan. That's better than eleven square miles. Closer to twelve square miles, and you want to steal it for five hundred dollars."

"I wouldn't call it stealing, exactly."

"Well, what would you call it?" He ducked the ash from his cigar and rolled the cigar between his thumb and forefinger. His hands were very large, the fingers blunt. "That's about thirty dollars for a square mile of land. Well, more than that. Let me figure a minute—"

He used a pencil and paper, calculated quickly, looked up in triumph. "Just a shade over forty dollars a square mile," he said. "That's pretty cheap, John. Now I wouldn't call that a high price."

"Neither would I."

"So?"

I took a breath. "But Barnstable's not looking to pay a high price," I said. I looked at him very sincerely. "We want to buy land cheaply, Wally. We can use this land—we have a client who's interested in a hunting preserve in that area, but we have to get that land at our price."

"When you figure my cost—"

"But at least this enables you to get out of it once and for all, and to cut your loss. Then too, once you've sold the land you can take your capital loss on it for tax purposes."

He thought that over. "I had an argument with my tax man on that a few years ago," he said slowly. "You know what the guy wanted me to do? Wanted me to sell the works to someone for a dollar. Just get rid of it for nothing so that I'd be transferring title and I could list a twenty-thousand-dollar loss. I couldn't see giving something away like that, not something like land. I'd rather keep the land and pay the damn taxes."

"Well, we would be paying you more than a dollar."

"Five hundred dollars, you mean."

"That's right."

He called the waitress over and ordered another Scotch and water. I joined him. He remained silent until the girl brought the drinks. It was past one now, and the lunch crowd had thinned down considerably. He sipped his drink and put it down on the table and looked at me.

"I'll tell you something," he said. "At that price I just wouldn't be interested."

"I'm sorry to hear that."

"But I think you'll have trouble finding anyone who'll be inclined to take the kind of offer you've made me."

"There's a lot of land up in that neck of the woods," I said.

"Yes, I know that."

"And we've had little difficulty buying it at our price so far," I went on, and then stopped abruptly and studied the tablecloth in front of me.

"You're interested in more than just my land, then."

"Well, that's not what I meant to say. Of course we've bought occasional parcels of this type of property before, but—"

"For hunting lodges."

"Actually, no. But we've had occasion to purchase unimproved land in the past, and in cases like this, we're usually able to get the land at a low price. When you're dealing with worthless land—"

"No land is useless."

"Well, of course not."

His eyes probed mine. I met his glance for a moment, then averted my eyes. When I looked back he was still scanning my face.

"This is beginning to interest me," he said finally.

"I had hoped it would."

"And one thing that interests me is that you haven't upped your offer. I figured from the beginning that if you would open with an offer of five hundred you'd be prepared to go to double that. But you haven't given me any of the usual runaround, about calling the home office and trying to get them to raise the ante. None of that. You've just about got me convinced that five hundred is as high as you intend to go."

"It is."

"Uh-huh. Anything important happening in Canada that I don't know about?"

"I don't understand."

"I mean that it would be quite a joke if it turned out that there really was uranium on that land, wouldn't it?"

"I assure you—"

"Oh, I'm sure there isn't." I was obviously uncomfortable, and he was enjoying this. "I'm sure the land is just as rotten and deserted as it always was. But I am interested, and not so much in your offer as in what lies beneath it. That's something that I find very interesting."

"Well," I said.

He finished his drink and put the glass down. "This whole situation is something I'd like to give a certain amount of thought to. Five hundred dollars is an almost immaterial factor here as far as I'm concerned. The question is what I want to do with the land, whether or not I want to own it. You can appreciate that."

"Then you might consider selling?"

"Oh, yes," he said. He was not very convincing. "But the thing is, I want to think it over. Were you planning to stay overnight in Olean?"

"I was going to fly back this evening."

"You ought to stay," he said. "I'll tell you, I'd like to have dinner with you tonight. I have to get moving now, I'm late for an appointment as it is, but I'd like to go over this with you and perhaps get a fuller picture. It might be worth your while if you spent an extra day here."

"Well—"

"And there's a really fine restaurant out on Route 17. Marvelous food. Could you stay?"

He talked me into it. He signaled the waiter and took the check. I didn't fight him for it.

I divided the rest of the afternoon between a barbershop down the street from the hotel and a tavern next door to the barbershop where I nursed a Würzburger and watched a ball game on television. When I got back to the hotel there was a message for me to call Mr. Gunderman. I went to my room and called him.

"Glad I reached you, John. Listen, I'm in a bind as far as tonight is concerned. There's a fund-raising dinner that I'm involved in and it slipped my mind completely this afternoon. Then I thought I could get out of it but it turns out that I can't. They've decided that I'm the indispensable man or something."

"That's too bad," I said. "I was looking forward to it."

"So was I." He paused, then swung into gear. "I'll tell you—I really did want to see you, and now I've gone and gotten you to stay over and all. How would it be if I sent my secretary to sub for me? I don't know if you noticed, but she's easy on the eyes."

"I noticed."

He chuckled. "I can imagine. Now look—you don't have a car, do you?"

"No, I flew in and then took a cab. I could have rented a car there, I suppose, but I didn't bother."

"Well, Evvie drives. She'll pick you up at your hotel at six, is that all right? And then you and I can get together in the morning."

"That sounds fine," I said.

I spruced up for my date. I remembered the dark brown hair and the brown eyes and the shape of that long tall body, and I combed my newly trimmed hair very carefully and splashed a little after-shave gunk on my face. I took off the blue tie and put on one with a little more authority to it.

There was a Western Union office down the block, sandwiched in between the Southern Tier Realty Corp. and a small loan company. I got a message blank and sent a wire collect to Mr. Douglas Rance at the Barnstable Corporation, 3119 Yonge Street, Toronto, Ontario, Canada.

I wired: ALL GOES WELL. PROSPECT DUBIOUS AT FIRST BUT HAVE HOPES OF SUCCESSFUL TRANSACTION. STAYING OLEAN OVERNIGHT. JOHN HAYDEN.

Then I went back to the Olean House to wait for Evvie.

Two

It was the tail end of July when Doug Rance dropped around to see me. I didn't even recognize him at first. It had been a good eight or nine years since we had seen each other, and we were never close, never worked together. Now he was about thirty-three to my forty-two. Before, when I'd known him, he was just a raw kid and I was an old hand.

It was a Wednesday night, around twelve-thirty. I was working the four-to-midnight swing at the Boulder Bowl, and the night had been a slow one. The bowling leagues ease off during the summer months and open bowling only gets a heavy play on the weekends. By eleven-thirty the place was just about empty. I rolled a pair of unimpressive games, helped the kid with the mop-up, and made a note for Harry to call AMF in the morning and tell them one of their automatic pin-spotters had died on us. I locked up a few minutes after twelve, had a short beer around the corner, and walked the rest of the way to my room on Merrimac.

When I got there, Rance was waiting for me. He was sitting on a chair with his legs crossed, smoking a cigarette. He got up when I walked in and gave me a large grin.

"The door was open," he said.

"I don't lock it."

I was trying to place him. He was about my height with a lot of curly black hair and a smile that came easy. A very good-looking guy. Ladies'-man looks. He crossed the room and stuck out his hand and I took it.

"You don't make me, do you? It's been a while."

And then I did. The first image that jumped into my mind was of a young, good-looking guy standing up straight and listening pop-eyed while Ray Warren and Pappy Lee bragged about a sweet chickie-bladder con they had pulled off in Spokane. He wasn't that young now, or that fresh. Well, neither was I.

"You're looking good," he said.

"Well, thanks."

We stood around looking at each other for a few seconds. Then he said, "Say, I picked up a bottle around the corner. I didn't know what you're drinking these days but I got Scotch. Is that okay?"

"It's fine."

"If you've got a couple glasses—"

I found two water glasses and went down the hall to the john and rinsed them out. He poured a few fingers of Cutty Sark into them and we sat down. He took the chair, I stretched out on the bed and put my feet up. It was good Scotch.

I asked him how he'd found me.

"Well, I was in Vegas, Johnny. I asked around, and somebody said you were here in Boulder. Something about your working at a bowling alley. I went over to the place but I didn't want to bother you. One of the kids told me where you were living and I came on over."

"Why did you come?"

"To see you."

"Just to talk over old times?"

He laughed. "Is that a bad idea?"

"It's a funny reason to come this far."

"I guess it is. No, I've got business with you, Johnny, but let's let it wait for now. I was surprised as hell when they told me you were here. I've never been to Colorado before. You like it here?"

"Very much."

"How'd you happen to pick it?"

I told him I'd grown up not far from here, just across the border in New Mexico, a smallish town called Springer. "Like elephants, I guess. Going home to die."

"Nothing wrong with you, is there?"

"No, I was just talking." I worked on the Scotch. "I would have gone to New Mexico, maybe, but I've got a record there and it didn't seem like a good idea. This is about the same kind of country."

"A hell of a lot of mountains. I flew to Denver and drove up in a Hertz car. Mountains and open spaces."

"You can get pretty hungry for open spaces."

"Yes, I guess you can. Was it very bad, Johnny?"

"Yes, it was very bad." He offered me a cigarette. I took it and lit it. "It was very bad," I said.

"I can imagine."

"Have you ever been inside?"

"Three times. Twice for thirty days, once for ninety."

"Then you can't imagine," I said. "Then you can't have the vaguest goddamned idea about it."

He didn't say anything. I reached for the bottle and he gave it to me. I poured a lot of Scotch in my glass and looked at it for a few seconds before drinking it. I felt like talking now. I'd been out for eight months, and ever since I got out of California I hadn't run across anybody who was with it. Conversation with straight people is limited—you can't talk about the library at San Quentin, or about the first long con you worked, or about any of the things that made up your life for so many years. You can drink with them and gab with them, but you have to keep a lid on the major portion of yourself.

"I was in Q," I said. "I did seven years. You couldn't know what it was like. I didn't know, not until I was in. San Quentin's a model prison, you know. Recreational facilities, a good library, and the guards don't beat you up at night. There's only one thing wrong with the place. There's this cell, and there are these iron bars, and they lock that door and you have to stay inside. That's all. You have to stay inside.

"I drew ten-to-twenty. It was a sort of variation on the badger game and there was long green in it. The girl fakes a pregnancy and then there's a fake abortion and a fake death, and the mooch winds up with the hook in him all the way up to his liver. Only this time the whole play turned sour and we bought it, but good. I drew ten-to-twenty for grand larceny and extortion and a half a dozen other counts I don't remember."

"And got out in seven."

I finished the Scotch. "Seven years and three months. I could have made it a year earlier if I'd put in for parole."

"You didn't?"

"I didn't want it. Parole is a leash—you get out a little sooner but you have to stay on that leash, you have to report to some son of a bitch once a month, you have to stay in the state, you have to live like a mouse. I stayed very straight inside. I made every day's worth of good time I could make. I never got in trouble. But I didn't want parole. I didn't want any leash on me that could yank me back any time somebody decided I belonged inside again. I'm out now and I'm staying out. Nothing gets me back in again."

He didn't say anything. He filled our glasses. I put out my cigarette and got up from the bed and walked over to the window. There were a lot of stars out. I watched them and said, "I guess you made a trip for nothing, Doug."

"How's that?"

"Because I'm not interested."

He got up and came over and stood beside me. "You didn't even wait for the pitch."

"That's because I know I'm not swinging."

"It's a beautiful set-up, Johnny."

"They always are."

"This one's gilt-edged. All triple-A, front to back. The least you ought to do is hear about it."

"I don't think I want to."

He didn't say anything for a few minutes. We both worked on our drinks. He sat down on the chair again and I got back on the bed. When he started in again he came through from a new direction.

"You're some kind of manager at the bowling alley, Johnny?"

"Assistant manager."

"Sounds pretty good."

"Not really."

"The pay pretty decent?"

"Eighty-five a week. I should get raised to a hundred by the end of the year, and then it levels off."

"Well, that's not too bad."

I didn't say anything. He looked around at the room, which was not very impressive. I paid eight a week for it and the price fit the accommodations. I said, "But there's no bars on the windows, and nobody locks me in at night."

He grinned. "Sorry," he said. "Listen, I didn't mean to pry, but I couldn't help catching the stuff on your dresser. What's doing, some kind of a course?"

"I'm taking a correspondence course in hotel management."

"Yeah?" He looked genuinely interested. He was pretty good at it. "Are those things any good?"

"This one isn't. I did a little studying at Q, hotel management and restaurant operation. I figured I'd follow it up now. The gaff on this deal is only fifty bucks, so I can't really get burned too badly."

"You're interested in that, huh?"

I nodded. "It's a good life, with the right set-up."

"You got any plans?"

"Nothing definite. There's a place west of the city that I like. A roadhouse with rooms upstairs and a couple of cabins in back. The location is perfect, it's right on a road that gets a lot of traffic and there's not much competition around. The owner doesn't know what to do with the place. He's a lush and he just knows how to sell drinks and how to build himself a case of cirrhosis. With the right kind of operation the place would be a gold mine."

"You sound as though you've thought about it. What would you want to do, manage the place?"

"I'd want to own it."

"Is it for sale?"

"It would be, if anybody wanted it. Right now it looks like a losing proposition, because it's not being run the way it should be. A person could swing the deal with ten thou in cash and good terms for the rest. Then you would need another ten to put into the place, and a contingency fund of at least five more. Say twenty-five thousand, thirty at the outside, and a man could have a place that would go like a rocket."

"Is this place far from here?"

"A few miles. Why?"

"I'd like to have a look at it."

I looked at him and started to laugh. "Now what the

hell," I said. "You're hustling me pretty hard, aren't you, fella?"

"Maybe. Is the place open now? We could take a run over there and grab a drink. My car's right outside."

"Why?"

"Why not?"

He had a rented Corvair parked two doors down the block on the other side of the street. Bannion's was about three miles south and west of the town. There were half a dozen cars in the lot when we got there, eight or ten customers inside, all but two of them at the bar. Bannion didn't have a waitress working. We got our drinks at the bar and took them to a table in the back. We stayed there for about fifteen or twenty minutes. Three of the customers left while we were there. Nobody else came in.

I did most of the talking. The place had tremendous possibilities. Bannion had completely ignored the tourist business, and the only people who rented his rooms were couples looking for a quick roll in the hay. Hot pillow trade was always worthwhile for a place like that, but tourist trade was good, too, especially with all the skiers in the winter and all the vacationers in the summer.

The food potential was good, too. The place needed extensive renovation and remodeling, but the physical plant itself was ideal. I talked a blue streak. Rance couldn't have cared less, but he knew enough to seem interested and I was interested enough myself to go on talking whether he gave a damn or not.

On the way back to my place he said, "Well, you sold me. You could make a go of it there."

"More than a go. I could do damned well."

"And you need how much bread? Twenty-five thousand?"

"Thirty would be better. I could probably do it on twenty-five, but that's squeezing."

"Got anything saved?"

"Not much." I lit a cigarette. "I'm saving money. You saw the room I live in. I make eighty-five a week and take home a little better than seventy after deductions. I live cheap. No car, low rent. I can save half my pay with no trouble at all."

"And you need twenty-five or thirty."

"Uh-huh."

I let it go at that. If I saved twenty-five hundred a year, it would take me almost nine years, counting interest, to save twenty-five thousand dollars. He could manage that kind of arithmetic as well as I could, and I didn't like to spend too much time thinking about those figures. They didn't do much for my enthusiasm. They transformed all the plans to the approximate level of prison dreams. *When I'm outside I'm going to own eight liquor stores and ten whorehouses and sleep all day.* That kind of scene.

He parked the car and came back up to the room with me. He said, "I'd like to outline this grift for you."

"But I'm not on the grift any more. Why draw me pretty pictures?"

"I looked at your dream. Why not listen to mine?"

"We'd be wasting time. You won't even tempt me."

"Can't I try?"

"I hate like hell to be hustled, Doug."

"Who doesn't?" His face relaxed in that easy smile again. "Look at it this way—I made a trip for nothing. That was the chance I took, right? I came unannounced because I wanted to see you. I have this thing hanging fire and I wanted you in it with me."

"Why me?"

"Because you'd be only perfect for it. But the hell with that for the time being. The point is that I'm here, I made the trip, and if I can't get you in it with me I could at least get you to give the thing a listen and tell me how you think it would play. You've been a lot of years on the long con, Johnny."

"Too many years."

"Well, a long time. You were an old hand when I was still heating up zircons and selling them as diamonds to jewelers who didn't know better. I'm just getting into the big play."

"Who've you worked with?"

"I was up in Oregon. Portland. I was with Red Jamison and Phil Fayre and some other guys. I don't know if you know them." I knew Red and Phil. "We had this wire, it was the first job I worked with an elaborate store arrangement. The first one where I had a big piece of the action."

"What did you do?"

"I was inside. Red did the roping, Phil and I and half the people on the Coast were inside the store. We took this wholesale druggist for seventy-five thou and a few other mooches for ten or twenty apiece. It was beautiful the way it worked. The whole thing, the bit about a man at the track with a transistor set-up that got the results before the store did. It all worked like a beautiful piece of machinery. It was sweet."

He told me all about it. The wire con is one of the three standard long cons, and as old as you can get. You keep being surprised when it still works after all those years. He told me all the cute little details and I could tell just how much of a kick it was for him, a kick to pull it off, a kick to remember it and talk about it. In a lot of ways he was the same kid I'd known before, in love with the whole pattern of the life, in love with the whole idea of being with it. I tried to remember if I had been like that once, all enthusiasm and excitement. It didn't seem possible.

"But that's history," he said. "Let me tell you what I've got on the stove now. You know the Canadian moose pasture bit, don't you?"

"I worked it once."

"That's what I heard. How did you work it? Stock?"

"Uranium stocks."

"You've heard it worked with land?"

"I know somebody was doing it that way somewhere in the East. It's the same thing, isn't it?"

"Just about," he said. "It's also just about played out, although there are still a few boiler rooms going in Toronto. I was inside of one with half a dozen phones going full-time."

"Is that what you want to set up?"

He laughed. "No, this is nothing like that. This is quicker and neater and easier and the score is a lot bigger. This is a fresh wrinkle on the whole thing. I'll tell you, Johnny, this is one I dreamed up all by myself. I heard this girl's story—"

"What girl?"

"A girl I met in Vegas. I'll get to that. I heard her story, and I got a picture of this mooch in my mind, and I just let it lay around there. I wasn't in Vegas to line up a con and I wasn't there for a woman, either. I never pull a job in Vegas, or anywhere else in the state. That place is strictly for gambling for me."

"You gamble a lot?"

"I'm a high roller when I'm not working. Everybody has a weakness, Johnny. On the con or off it, everybody has one thing that gets to him. Women or liquor or gambling or something. The trouble is when you've got more than one vice. You know, I'm getting way off the track here. Let me just give you a fast picture. It's getting late and all, and you must be pretty beat, and I'm not so bright-eyed and bushy-tailed myself. I'll just sketch it in for you."

He gave me just the outline. He ran through it very quickly, very sketchily. He knew what he was doing. He was working me the same way you work a mark at the beginning, the same way a fisherman works a trout. Just teasing, poking the bait around, giving a flash of it and then jerking it away before you can even make up your mind whether or not to bite. I knew I was being hustled. It didn't bother me.

For one thing, it was impossible to dislike Doug Rance. He was too genuinely charming. A confidence man has to have one of two things going for him. He can be so tremendously charming that the mark likes him at first meeting, or he can be so obviously honest and sincere that the mark trusts him from the opening whistle. If the mooch likes you, or if he trusts you, you are halfway home; the rest is just mechanics.

Doug made it on charm. I was the other way, I was a man people were likely to trust. I don't know why this is so, but it is. I've always played things that way, pushing the honest-and-sincere bit, but you can't make it on acting talent alone.

Charm and sincerity. The best two-handed cons feature a pair of men who compliment one another in this respect, one of them charming and one of them sincere. Doug wanted me in this one, and he probably knew what he was doing in picking me. The odds were that we would work well together.

I let him get all the way through the pitch and I listened to him all the way. He skipped most of the details, so it was hard to tell if the thing was as good as it sounded right off the bat. There could be snags he hadn't thought of, rough spots he'd glossed over. On the surface, though, the thing looked beautiful.

"It's a new one," I told him.

"I thought it was."

"Of course, I've been out of circulation for seven years. But I think you found something new."

"Do you like it?"

"Yes," I said. And lit a cigarette and added, "But I'm afraid it's not for me. I'm just not buying."

"Oh, I know," he said easily. "I just wanted your opinion. I wish I could have you in on it, but you can't win them all." He got to his feet. "I'm going to split, Johnny. I'm halfway dead. I've got a room over at the Mountain Lodge."

"Where do you go from here?"

"I'm not sure. I figure I'll be in town until tomorrow night, anyway. Maybe we'll get together, huh?"

What a sweet soft hustler he was. I stood up. "Drop around. We'll have lunch."

"Fine."

When he had his hand on the knob I gave him the first nibble. The words just came out by themselves. What I said was, "Just for curiosity, how big do you think you'd score on this one?"

He pretended to think. "Hard to say. I know what I figured your end at."

"Oh?"

"About thirty thou," he said.

Three

I tried not to think about it. I listened as his car pulled away, and I blocked out the echo of his parting line, and I got undressed and crawled into bed and found out in no time at all that I wasn't going to drop off to sleep all that easily. I flipped the light back on and killed some time working on my correspondence course homework. Actually I was taking two courses at once, one in hotel and restaurant management and one in basic accounting. I worked out four of the accounting problems before my eyes started backing up on me. I lit a fresh cigarette and sat down on the edge of the bed.

So I thought about some of the things I hadn't wanted to think about. Like how long it would take to save thirty thousand dollars, and how old I would be when I had it. Fifty at the earliest, and probably a lot more like fifty-five. I was forty-two, and forty-two was still young enough for big plans and hard work, but fifty—well, fifty was a lot closer to being old. And fifty-five was closer still.

I thought about spending another ten years in that little room, scrimping and saving to beat hell. Adding up score sheets at the Boulder Bowl, grabbing quick lunches at diners and coffee pots. Dreaming through correspondence courses.

I had liked that life, too. But a man can endure many things day by day that become unthinkable when seen as a larger chunk of time. My life was all right as long as I lived it a day at a time. See it as ten years of the same thing, with Bannion selling his place to somebody else somewhere along the line, with the dream evaporating and the correspondence courses discontinued and nothing left but the habit; work and sleep and save. See it that way and the window grows bars and the door locks itself and the eight-dollar room turns itself into a cell.

Doug had left the bottle of Cutty. I let it alone. Dawn was breaking by the time I managed to get to sleep. I did not sleep well, I did not sleep long. There were dreams I don't remember. Around nine o'clock I woke up, chilled and damp, certain at first that I was not here in my room in Boulder but back in my cell at San Quentin.

I showered, I shaved, I smoked. If only there was something really wrong with his grift, I thought. If only there was a pretty snag I could catch around my finger. If only I could see the flaw. But on the surface it looked too very perfect, with a big payoff for maybe three months of work, and with no chance at all of a foul-up that could lead me back to a cell.

Rance showed up at eleven-thirty. "I'm catching a four o'clock plane from Denver," he said. "I'll have to drive back there. Let's grab lunch now."

"Come on in and sit down."

"Oh?"

"I want to hear the whole thing," I said. "It sounded too damned good last night. I want to prove that there's something wrong with it."

"And if there isn't?"

"Well."

He took it from the top. It went back five years to a time when a few of the New York boys were working a boiler-room operation out of Toronto. It was a standard high-pressure operation with one important difference. Instead of peddling uranium or oil stocks, or mineral rights, the promoters were selling parcels of raw land itself. They bought up the land for thirty to fifty cents an acre and sold it for three or four dollars an acre.

"Goldin and Prince were on top of this one," he said. "You've got to remember when this was, just five years ago. The uranium stock con got its first big play right after the war, and then it came back strong during the Korean thing and for about a year after that. By the time it ran its course everybody had a little bell inside his head that rang when you mentioned the words *Canadian uranium stocks*. The newspapers and magazines ran features on the con and Washington circulated lists of bad stocks and everybody got wise, even the thickest marks around. But Goldin and Al Prince had a gimmick working for them. They weren't selling stocks. They were pushing the land itself, and that let the mark see that he was getting something. You tell him he can buy a thousand acres of valuable land for three or four thousand dollars and he doesn't see how he can get taken. The land is real, it's there for him to look at. Half the time he doesn't know what a thousand acres is. All he knows is that it's a lot of land. It's maybe four hundred dollars worth of land that he's paying ten times actual value for, but he doesn't know this."

I said it was expensive—Goldin and Prince had to buy the land in the first place, and that cost more than printing up stock certificates.

"They didn't care. They were operating on the mooches' money, buying the land after they'd collected, and they didn't mind knocking ten percent off the top to cover the cost of the land itself. Besides, the whole thing came out perfectly legal. They promised land and they delivered land, and any extra promises were verbal and uncollectable. It worked for them. They sold half of Canada, or close to it. Northern Alberta and Saskatchewan, some tracts in the Yukon and in the Northwest Territories."

I told him to go on. "All right," he said. "That's the background. Now you've got a bunch of marks around the country who own land they paid maybe ten times too much for. They're stuck with it. Right?"

"Right."

"Good. Now we skip to this frail I found in Vegas. She's a secretary in her late twenties. For the past six years or so she's been working for this millionaire. For about four of those years she's been sleeping with him. All this time his wife was sick. She thought he was going to marry her when the wife finally died. A year ago the wife died."

"And he didn't marry her."

"Didn't and doesn't plan to. She's not too happy about this. She's a good-looking broad; she was married once before and the marriage fell in. Now she's stuck in a hick town working for this guy and she'd like to get the hell away from him and make a good marriage. She figures that she needs front money to do this. She wants to marry rich, and that means going where the money is and living the part. She'd like to pick up a healthy piece of change, and she'd also like to stick it into this guy and break it off, because she figures he has it coming."

"She really expected him to marry her?"

"Yes. She was bitching about him and I started drawing her out just automatically, and she gave me a good picture of the guy. That started the wheels turning. You can see how it went. I said something about how she'd probably like to see him get taken but good, and she mentioned that he had been taken once before, when she had just started working for him. And of course it was this Canadian deal that had hooked him. He bought a nice stretch of mooseland from Capital Northwestern Development, which was what Goldin and Prince were calling themselves about that time."

"How deep did he go?"

"Twenty or twenty-five thou."

"Jesus."

"Uh-huh. So now we come to the mooch himself. His name is Wallace J. Gunderman. He lives in some-place called Olean, in western New York near the Pennsylvania border. His father got rich in oil. Gunderman got richer in land. If he wasn't so rich you'd laugh all over him, because he'll buy any piece of land he can get at his price. He's a nut on the subject, according to what Evvie said."

"Evvie?"

"Evelyn Stone, that's her name. But Gunderman. He'll buy any piece of land, no matter how worthless it is. He started doing this about thirty years ago. He made out very well. Part of this was a matter of luck, of being in the right place at the right time and having the cash to operate on. Another part was shrewdness. He's supposed to be a tough man in a trade."

He went on about Gunderman. Five years ago Gunderman had gone for a minimum of twenty thousand dollars and had wound up with a chunk of scrubland with a fair market value in the neighborhood of two grand. He was rich enough to stand that sort of a loss without any trouble, but the whole thing hit him where he lived. He was proud of himself, of his head for business, and here he'd been taken in his own backyard, on a land swindle. This wasn't easy to live down. He still owned the land and he liked to tell people that he would make out on it eventually, that any land would be valuable if you held it long enough.

But he was itching to get the bad taste of that con out of his system. He had been crazy to take that kind of a beating. If he could wind up turning his loss into a profit, if he could make out nicely on that Canadian land, then he would wind up crazy like a fox.

"You can see where he stands, Johnny."

"Uh-huh."

"The right type of set-up—"

"And he's there with both hands full."

"That's the idea. And here's how it works, and this is all mine and I think it's beautiful. Gunderman gets a letter making him an offer for his Canadian land. This gets his head spinning right away. Nobody's ever been interested in this land and he can't understand why anybody would want it. What he probably figures from the go is that there's been a uranium strike in the neighborhood, or something like that, and he wants to find out what's up. He checks, and nothing's up, the land is as worthless as ever.

"Then you go to see him and repeat the offer. You—"

"What am I offering?"

"About five hundred dollars."

"For something that ran him twenty thou?"

"Right. Of course he doesn't take it. Then he finds out we've been making the same kind of offer to other men who got caught in the Capital Northwestern Development swindle. That stirs him up. It's not just his land, it's a whole lot of land that we're looking to buy. He can't figure out why, but two things are certain. First of all, he's not going to sell that land of his, not for anything. And second, he's going to be hungry to find things out."

Bit by bit we would let Gunderman figure things out. We wanted to buy his land for five hundred dollars because it was worth in the neighborhood of two thousand dollars, maybe as much as three. We were a group of important Canadians with a lot of legitimate interests who had managed to get hold of a list of men taken in by Capital Northwestern Development. We were attempting to buy their land from them at twenty to twenty-five percent of its fair market value. For around fifty thousand dollars we would be able to acquire title to a huge block of Canadian real estate worth close to a quarter of a million dollars, and with a tremendous potential for future price appreciation. A potential Gunderman could certainly understand— the investment value of unimproved land was his personal religion. The more he nosed around the more he learned about our operation, and the more he learned about it the more he liked it.

"So he doesn't want to sell us his land, Johnny. He wants to buy our land, the whole package." He lit a cigarette. "You like it so far, Johnny?"

I slipped the question. "If it's such an attractive deal, why would we be willing to sell it to him?"

"That's where it gets pretty. Remember what we're supposed to be. We're a syndicate of highly respectable Canucks who've hit on something a little sneaky. Legal, sure, but sneaky. We're capitalizing on an old con game and buying land surreptitiously for a fraction of its value. We're dealing with people who've been taken to the point where they think of their land as utterly worthless, and we're buying it in very cheap."

"And?"

"And we don't want to turn this into a long-term deal. We want to get in and get out, to take a quick but sweet profit and go about our business. You'll be working outside, getting tight with Gunderman. He'll figure out what a perfect man he'd be for us to deal with, taking this piece of land that ran us around fifty thousand and selling it to him for maybe double that. I figure we'd try for one-fifty and settle for an even hundred thou."

"Go on."

"Right. Now here is where Gunderman has to prove that we can trust him. We would be selling the land damned cheap at a hundred thou. We're willing to do that if we're sure of who we're dealing with. We can't afford the risk of selling to somebody who's going to turn around and dump it for a fast buck. We've got our personal reputations to consider. We've got to sell to the type of man who will sit on that land for a few years, letting it increase in value as far as that goes, and then sell right for a good price later on. That way we don't come out of it with our reputations in a sling.

"And of course this is perfect for Gunderman, because he wants the land for long-term investment, not for a fast deal. He'll sit on it for five years if he has to. We let him convince us of this, and then we sell to him, and that's all she wrote."

I wondered if Rance knew just how perfect it was. The trickiest part of any con game is the blow-off, when you've got the mooch's money and you want to get him out of the way before he tips to the fact that he's been taken. A blow-off can be very blunt or very subtle or anything in-between. In the short con games you can just blow your mark off against the wall, sending him around the corner while you jump in a cab and get out of the neighborhood. In a long con, you ought to do better than that. The longer it takes him to realize he's been had, the less chance there is that he'll squawk and the less chance that it'll do him any good.

This was tailored for a perfect blow-off. Our Mr. Gunderman might die of old age before he found out he didn't really own any land in Canada.

I said, "We don't sell him land. We sell him our company."

"Instead of faking deeds?"

"Sure. That way he never gets around to a title search or anything else. He buys a hundred percent of the stock of our corporation. He thinks the corporation owns certain real estate and it doesn't. I'll tell you something. I think the whole deal might even be legal. He'll be buying a corporation and he'll be getting a corporation. If there's nothing on paper—"

"Jesus, I think you're right."

By then I was hooked. I think I must have known it

myself. Once you start improving a scheme, building on it, smoothing it, you are damned well a part of it.

We had lunch at the Cattleman's Grill. Open steak sandwiches and cold bottles of ale. We let the deal alone during lunch. We found other things to talk about. Doug picked up the tab.

Afterward, we drove around in his car. I lit a cigarette and pitched the match out the window.

"About the money arrangement," I said.

"Uh-huh."

"How did you figure it?"

"I figured you in for thirty."

"Out of a hundred? That doesn't sound too wonderful."

"Well, it won't be a hundred, Johnny. We'll gross a hundred, but there are going to be some expenses that have to come out of the nut, and then there's twenty off the top for the girl. Now—"

"That's too damned much for the girl," I said.

"It can't be less."

"The hell it can't. She ought to be in for a finder's fee of five thou and no more. Why twenty?"

"Because she did more than set this up. She's going to be working this from the inside, right there in his office. She'll be in on the whole play, and she'll have to scoot after it's over. Besides, there has to be a big piece in it for her or she won't go. She wants a stake to go hunt a husband with, and if it's not enough of a stake she'll get shaky and pull out."

I let that ride. "So how did you figure the split?"

"Twenty off the top, plus maybe ten more off the top for expenses, leaves seventy. I figured forty and thirty."

"What's wrong with evens?"

The smile stayed. "Well, it is my job, Johnny."

I knew it wasn't the five. This was the first con he was working from the top, and he needed the glory as much as the money. If we split it down the middle he didn't get as much of a boost out of it. We tossed it back and forth. I told him to pare the girl's end of it down to seventeen-five and to cut himself down to thirty-seven and a half and give me thirty-five even. He didn't like it that way. He said he'd chop her to seventeen-five and add her end to mine, keeping forty for himself.

"You can swing your deal with thirty easy, Johnny. Ten to buy the place, ten to fix it up, and ten more in reserve. Two and a half more is just gravy."

So we settled it that way. Forty thousand dollars for him, thirty-two thousand, five hundred for me, seventeen thousand and a half for Evelyn Stone. The extra twenty-five hundred wasn't really important to me as money. It was a question of face. We agreed that anything over and above the hundred thou would be split down the middle between us, with the girl out of it.

I said, "We're going to need front money."

"I've got the bankroll."

"How much?"

"Close to ten grand."

"I'd feel better with double that. But ten should do

us without much sweat. I've got a few hundred set aside. Living money, eating money."

"We can do it on ten."

"It might mean cutting it close. The more you can spend on your front the better off you are. And sometimes it isn't even a question of spending it, it's having it in the bank. Oh, the hell. Where do we kick this off from? Toronto?"

"That's where our store will be. Our company."

"Then there's no worry. Unless something happened to him. Do you know Terry Moscato?"

He didn't.

"Well, he ought to be all right. He wouldn't be in jail, he's in too good to take a fall. He used to work out on the Coast and then he went East and wound up in Toronto, and he'll loan us front money. It has to be strictly front money, dough that sits in a bank account in our name and that goes straight back to him as soon as we're out of it. We'll have to pay a thousand for the use of ten, but it's worth it."

"See why I wanted you on this, Johnny?" He took a hand from the wheel and punched me gently on the knee. "I never would have thought of an angle like that. The extra touches. But I'll learn them, kid."

I wasn't listening. It was that old familiar feeling, getting into it, getting with it again, feeling your mind start to slip into gear. Funny after so many years. *The extra touches.* A whole batch of them were coming to me now. The hell with it, we could talk about them later.

"I'll need eight days," I told him.

"For what?"

"One day to decide if I'm in. And a week's notice before I leave my job."

"I thought you already decided you were in."

"I want twenty-four hours to make sure."

He shrugged this off. "And a week's notice? That's a new one. You're not going to come back and play assistant manager anymore, Johnny. What the hell do you care about giving notice?"

"The same reason you don't do any grifting in Nevada. I don't crap where I eat."

"Oh."

"I'll be coming back to this town," I said. "Not as a flunky, no, but to live here and do business here. I want to leave it right."

I spent the hour before I started work on the telephone. I sat in a booth at a drugstore and kept pouring change down the slot. I called a lot of people that I couldn't reach and reached a lot of others. I spent my dinner hour at the telephone, and I got back on the phone that night after I left the alleys. I spoke to people who knew Doug Rance vaguely, to some who knew him well, to one or two who had worked with him not long ago.

You damn well have to know who's working with you. When you're all wrapped up in a big one you live a whole slew of lies all at once, and if you have a few people in on it who are lying back and forth and

conning each other as much as they're conning the
mooch, then you are looking for trouble and fairly certain of finding it. This doesn't mean that good con men
are inherently honest in their dealings among themselves. They aren't. If they were honest, they wouldn't
have gone on the C to begin with. I expected Doug
would lie to me, and I expected to lie to Doug, but not
to the point where we'd be fouling each other up. If
there were things I ought to know about him, I wanted
to know them now.

He checked out pretty well. They knew him in
Vegas, all right. He was a high roller, an almost com-
pulsive gambler, but he never gambled while he
worked. On a job, he was nothing but business. I had
wondered about that.

He was in love with the life, which was another
thing I had managed to figure out by myself. He was
good and he was smooth. He was attractive to women
but he could generally take them or leave them. He'd
done a short bit in a county jail in Arizona, and he'd
done time twice in California, a vag charge in Los
Angeles and a ninety-day stretch at Folsom for petty
theft, a short con that hadn't worked right.

Everyone I talked to, everyone who knew him,
seemed to like him well enough. That much figured.
That was his stock in trade.

It was another late night for me, but this time I
slept. In the morning I walked over to his hotel and we
had a bite together. He asked me if I'd had a chance to
run a check on him.

"Sure."

"How did I make out?"

"You've got good references."

He laughed. "I'm glad you asked around," he said. "I'd hate to work with anyone who wouldn't take the trouble. You in, Johnny?"

"All the way."

"You won't regret it. Smooth as silk, all the way, and nothing's going to go sour on us."

I gave notice that afternoon. I told Harry that I had to leave at the end of next week, that I had a very attractive opportunity waiting on the East Coast and I couldn't afford to pass it up. He was unhappy. He told me he could maybe see his way clear to a ten-a-week raise if I cared to stay. I told him it wasn't that, that this was a real chance for me.

"Maybe you'll come back some day," he said. "Not to work here, maybe, but to open up a place of your own. This is a good place to live, John."

"I'd like to come back."

"Hope you do. I hate to lose you, I really do."

Four

That was Friday. The following night I finished work at midnight. I had Sunday off, so Doug picked me up after work and we drove to Denver. He gave the Corvair back to the Hertz people. We caught a jet to Chicago, changed planes and flew on to Toronto. We spent Sunday renting apartments. He took a two-room place in a good building, and I booked a sixty-a-month room in a residential hotel on Jarvis near Dundas. I paid a month's rent on the place. We picked out a spot for our offices, rented them Monday morning in Doug's name. Then I flew back to Denver.

By that Thursday Harry had found a man to replace me at the alleys. I spent a few hours that afternoon breaking him in, then went back to my room and threw a few things into a suitcase. I had cleared out my bank account and I had the money in cash, something like eight hundred bucks and change. I threw out some of my clothes along with my correspondence course debris and other odds and ends. Then I was on another plane, headed again for Toronto by way of Chicago.

By this time Doug had set some of the wheels in motion. He found us a Richmond Street lawyer who was handling the incorporation procedures for us. Doug gave him a list of tentative names—Somerset, Stonehenge, and Barnstable, all of them crisply Anglo-Saxon. Our lawyer checked them out and discovered that there was already a Somerset Mining and Smelting, Ltd., and a Stonehenge Development, Ltd. Our third choice was open. The lawyer filled out an application for letters-patent for the Barnstable Corporation, Ltd., and shot it off to the Lieutenant-General of the Province of Ontario.

All of this was routine. We incorporated with two hundred shares of stock of a par value of one dollar. We stated our corporate purpose on our application, listing ourselves as organizing for the purpose of purchasing and developing land in the western provinces. We gave the address of our head offices as 3119 Yonge Street, Toronto. We listed three officers—Douglas Rance, President; Claude P. Whittlief, Vice-President and Treasurer; and Phillip T. Liddell, Secretary. Liddell was our lawyer. Whittlief was me—just another hat to wear, another name to sign. We gave our capitalization as fifty thousand dollars, Canadian. You don't have to show your capital, just proclaim it. Fifty seemed like a decent figure.

The charter went through and we were the Barnstable Corporation, Ltd., with a charter from the Province to prove it. We painted that name on the door of the Yonge Street office and had the phone company put in a bank of telephones. A printer on Dundas ran off a ream of stationery on good high rag content bond. Our incorporation was duly listed in the appropriate section of the Ontario *Gazette*.

We opened an account at one of the downtown offices of the Canadian Imperial Bank of Commerce. All checks on our account had to be signed by Rance and countersigned by me as Claude Whittlief. We deposited seventy-five hundred dollars of Doug's capital in the account. It wasn't enough of a balance. I went on the earie and found out that Terry Moscato had moved across the border to Buffalo. I flew down to see him and told him I needed ten thousand dollars for about two months, maybe three.

"For what?"

"Front money," I said. "It goes in a bank account and it stays there, Terry."

"Because I wouldn't want to be financing this at a lousy ten percent."

"Strictly front money, Terry."

Not that he trusted me, but he knew that I knew better than to play fast with him. People who crossed him had trouble getting insurance, and I was well aware of this, and that was enough collateral as far as he was concerned. I got ten grand from him in cash, bought a cashier's check for that amount at a bank, flew back to Toronto and stuck the money in the Barnstable account.

So we were in business.

A store is a vital element in the operation of a big con. It must look more like what it's pretending to be than the real article itself. The most difficult illusion to maintain is one of furious activity. The store—in our case, the office and the corporation itself—was geared for one thing and one thing only, the act of parting a certain fool from his money with a minimum of risk. But we had to give the appearance of conducting a full-fledged business. Our bank account had to show activity. Our office had to receive a sensible volume of mail.

Doug hired a secretary to answer the phone and type occasional letters. There were a variety of letters that we kept her busy with. Some of them were dictated just so she would have plenty of work. They never wound up in the mailbox. Carbons went in the files, and the letters themselves went in the trash barrel. Others were requests for catalogs and information, and these were duly mailed and brought mail in return.

Finally, we had her dash off a list of letters to men who had been swindled by Capital Northwestern Development. Doug Rance knew a man who knew Al Prince, and Al Prince supplied us with a master list of guppies he and Goldin had taken for a swim in the CND gambit. We picked some names off the list, carefully selecting men who had only lost between five hundred and two thousand dollars. We sent off letters on Barnstable stationery with Doug's signature offering to purchase their land for about three or four cents on the dollar, ostensibly for a hunting preserve, and stressing that their sale to us would enable them to take a tax loss and cut their losses on the deal.

"This doesn't make sense," Doug said. "Why in hell buy their land?"

I explained it to him. When we approached Gunderman, he would do a little checking on his own hook, and he would run down some of the men who had sold land to us and confirm that we were actually buying the property.

"The hell," he said. "That's no problem. He'll dictate his letters to Evvie and she'll sidetrack them."

"But she can let these go through," I told him, "and Gunderman will get actual confirmation. And we'll have actual deeds to show him along with the phony ones. The cash involved won't be much. A few dollars here and a few dollars there, and we won't sink more than a thousand at the outside into land."

"Does Gunderman get one of these letters?"

"No. Have the girl send him one, but don't mail it to him, mail it to our girl in his office. Let her sneak it into the files without showing it to him."

"So he can discover it later?"

"Right," I said.

What the hell—the girl was in on the play for seventeen-five. She might as well make herself useful.

We let our girl write up about thirty of those letters and we mailed out eight or ten of them. Two men wrote back immediately accepting our offer, and we sent them checks by return mail. Others wrote asking for more information, which we dutifully supplied. One of those later accepted our offer. One man said that he had already disposed of his land at a price slightly higher than our offer in order to take a tax loss. Two men wanted to get us to boost our offer, and we wrote back stating that our original offer had been firm and we couldn't possibly raise it. One of these men accepted, one didn't.

We wound up spending about three hundred dollars on moose pasture and got title to around twenty-nine hundred acres.

Activity in our bank account was even simpler to create. Doug would write checks to various persons. I countersigned the checks as Whittlief, then endorsed them on the back with the name of the nonexistent payee and put them through my own account, an account I'd taken out under the name of P. T. Parker. I cashed each check through the Parker account and redeposited the money in the Barnstable account. With a balance of between twelve and seventeen thousand dollars, we managed to show a turnover of around forty thousand dollars in the first month of operation, and the only cost to us was that of banking fees, which were small enough. Anyone who looked at our bank statement would see a record of steady activity with a lot of money coming in and a lot going out. Anybody looking at our corporate checkbook would see a wide variety of men and companies listed as payees for various checks. No one would uncover the fact that almost every one of those checks had gone through one P. T. Parker's account. Parker's name appeared on the cancelled checks, but we weren't showing those around.

✿

There was a lot of waiting to do. No matter how much activity we feigned, you couldn't get around the fact that we were stuck with leading fundamentally inactive lives until our front had had time to age and ripen a little. Fortunately we weren't trying to live the part of an old established firm. Part of our cover was that we had incorporated only recently, that the Barnstable outfit was an organization of sharpshooters set up on a short-term basis with a specific purpose.

All well and good, but we still had to be two months in operation before I could set about the business of roping Gunderman. This was still a remarkably short time. I've known cons who would set up a store in one city a year in advance, just letting it build up by itself while they made a living at something else or on the short con or working other gigs or whatever. Then the store would be waiting for them when they were ready to use it.

I knew a man named Ready Riley from Philadelphia—dead now, and I miss him—who was facing a sentence of ninety days for some misdemeanor. He got out on bail before sentencing and set up a perfect front for a very pretty swindle. His store was a fake gambling casino. He set all the wheels in motion, then got sentenced and did ninety days standing on his ear, and got out of jail and pulled off the con and left town with a fat wallet. He had already earned his nickname before that job, but he lived up to it then.

Well. We had ourselves two months to bum and I didn't have much to do. My room was a few steps up from the place I'd had in Boulder. I had a private bath, and the furniture was a little less decrepit. I couldn't spend too much time in the room because I was supposed to be working. I couldn't spend much time at the office because I was supposed to be the firm's contact man, meeting prospects and trying to buy their land. I couldn't see too much of Doug because I was supposed to be a hired hand, not someone he'd pick to run around with socially.

I saw a lot of movies. I did some shopping and bought clothes with Toronto labels. I spent enough nights at a jazz club on Yonge called The Friars so that they knew my face and what I liked to drink. I did a lot of reading. I knocked around a lot, got the feel of the city.

It was a good town. Toronto had a feeling of growth and progress to it that reminded me of the West Coast states. There was a lot of money in the city, and a lot of action. The night spots did a good business even in the middle of the week. They closed early, at one o'clock, but they drew well.

There were times when I had to remind myself that I was in a foreign country. The money was different, and it took a while to get used to two-dollar bills in wide circulation. The people had a slight accent that you could get used to in not much time. The differences were small ones, and mostly on the surface. If you dropped the whole city in the States, it would take you a few minutes before anything seemed out of place.

I did some drinking, but not too much of it. I moved around quite a bit. Now and then I found a girl, but those relationships were strictly short-term, begun at night and over by morning.

Doug had said that everyone was entitled to one weakness, and that his was gambling. He wasn't gambling on the job. If I had a weakness, it was probably women, but I wasn't indulging that weakness on the job either. A mechanical romp, yes. An affair, no. There were enough lies already to live up to, and I didn't want any complications.

And one night I met Doug for dinner and we wound up at a side table at The Friars and nursed Scotch on the rocks and listened to a good hard-bop group. He said, "I think we're ready. I think tomorrow. I talked to Evvie this afternoon and he's in town, and he doesn't have anything pressing for the next few days to get him sidetracked."

I didn't say anything. I looked at him, and for a change I saw tension lines in that lover-boy face. They didn't remain there long. A smile wiped them away.

"This is big, Johnny."

"Uh-huh."

"If you figure we ought to wait a while, about another week or two—"

He had managed to pick up elements of a Canadian

accent. It showed on certain words. *About* came out *aboat*. I still sounded the same as ever, but then I wasn't posing as a native. I was just a transplanted American.

"Now's as good a time as any."

"Good," he said. "There's a couple ways to get there. You go to Buffalo first, and then south to Olean. There's one plane a day from Buffalo to Olean, or you can do it by bus or train. I think the bus is a better bet than the train."

"I'd rather fly."

"That's what I figured, and it makes more sense that you'd fly down for the meeting instead of wasting that time on a bus or a train. You fly American to Buffalo airport and then get a Mohawk flight to Olean, I wrote it out for you."

He left a few minutes after that. I stayed around for another drink, then walked back to my hotel. I knew I would have trouble getting to sleep. It was more trouble than I'd expected. I kept on thinking of the two bad things that could happen. I could hit a snag at the start, or I could rope him in neatly and then have a wheel come off later in the game.

If it blew up in the beginning, we were out two months' time and the money we'd spent so far. This was a tailor-made con. Gunderman might have been the only man on earth we were primed for, and if he tipped right off the bat we could junk the whole operation and forget it. Rance was out his stake, and I could flush away my plans for turning Bannion's road-house into a Rocky Mountain Grossinger's.

If it soured later on, we were out more than time and money. If it soured later on, we would go to jail.

I kept dreaming about that. About being locked away, locked up in a cell. I kept waking up in a sweat and sitting around smoking a cigarette and dropping off to sleep again and waking up out of another dream.

The next night I puddle-jumped to Olean. That night I slept well. And woke up, and met my mooch and tossed that lasso around his manly shoulders.

And waited now, in the lobby of the Olean House, for Evvie Stone.

Five

She was five or ten minutes late. I waited for her in the lobby. I sat in a red leather chair in front of the empty fireplace and kept glancing over at the doorway. She came through the door and got about a third of the way to the desk, and I stood up and walked across the lobby to meet her.

"Oh, Mr. Hayden," she said.

"Miss Stone."

"I had to double-park out in front, so if you're ready—"

We left the hotel together. Her car was a white Ford with a small dent in the right front fender. We got in and she spun a very neat U-turn, took a right on State Street and headed the Ford out of town on Route 17. She kept her eyes on the road.

I kept mine on her. She'd changed her clothes for dinner. Now she wore a very simple black dress with a scoop neckline. A green heart hung from a small gold chain around her throat, a very deep green against her white skin. Jade, I guessed. Her arms were bare, her hands very sure on the wheel.

"I'm supposed to be very nice to you," she said suddenly.

"I think I'll like that."

We stopped for a light and she turned to look at me. Her eyes were larger than I had remembered them, and deeper in tone. "You surprised the hell out of me this morning," she said. "You don't look like a confidence man."

"That's an asset."

"Yes, I'm sure it must be." The light changed. "Mr. Gunderman doesn't have an important engagement tonight, you know. He just decided that I'd learn more from you than he would."

"I guessed that. His idea or yours?"

"Well, he probably thinks he thought of it himself. I guess I actually led him into it. He told me he wished he could get more of a line on you, and that he was having dinner with you tonight, but that he didn't think you'd be too keen on opening up to him. I said that a girl could probably draw you out a lot better, and I said something about the way you looked at my legs before. You did look at my legs, you know."

"I know."

"I told him this, and he paced around the room and asked me how I'd like to have dinner with you. I let him talk me into it. I'm supposed to give you the full treatment. Dinner at The Castle at a cozy table for two, and then some quiet spot for drinks, and then you'll tell me secrets. You'll let me dig all the information about the Barnstable operation out of you."

"I might just do that."

"This is the place," she said suddenly. "Isn't it incredible?"

She pulled off the road to the right. There are probably as many restaurants in the country called *The Castle* as there are diners named *Eat*, but this was the first one I'd ever come across that looked the part. It was a sprawling brick-and-stone affair with towers and fortifications and pillars and gun turrets, everything but a moat, and all of this in a one-floor building. A medieval ranch house with delusions of grandeur.

"Wait until you see the inside, John."

"It can't live up to this."

"Wait."

Inside, there was a foyer with a fountain, a Grecian statue type of thing with water streaming from various orifices. The floor was tile, the walls all wood and leather, with rough-hewn beams running the length of the ceiling. The maître d' beamed his way over to us, and Evvie said something about Mr. Gunderman's table, and we were passed along to a captain and bowed through a cocktail lounge and a large dining room into something called the Terrace Room. The tables were set far apart, the lighting dim and intimate.

We ordered martinis. "You might as well order big," she told me. "He'll be unhappy if I don't give you the full treatment. This is a quite a place, isn't it? You don't expect it in Olean. But they have people who come from miles away to eat here."

"They couldn't make out just with local trade."

"Hardly. The place seats over eight hundred. There are rooms and more rooms. And the food is very good. I think our drinks are coming."

The martinis were cold and dry and crisp. We had a second round, then ordered dinner. She touted the chateaubriand for two and I rode along with it.

"I get called Evvie," she said. "What do I call you?"

"John will do."

"Doug Rance referred to you as Johnny."

"That's his style. He'd love it if he could call me the Cheyenne Kid, as far as that goes."

"Is that where you're from? Cheyenne?"

"Colorado, now. Originally New Mexico."

"That's what Wally said, but I didn't know whether you'd been telling him the truth or not. You've got him on the hook, John. You really have him all hot and bothered."

"That's what I thought."

"What happened at lunch?"

I ran through it for her and she nodded, taking it all in. She was all wrapped up in the play herself. Usually I hate having an amateur in on things too deeply, but she seemed to have a feeling for the game. It wasn't necessary to tell her things twice. She listened very intently with those brown eyes opened very wide and she hung on every word.

"He was hopping when he got back to the office," she said. "He was on the phone most of the day, and he dictated a batch of letters to me. Do you want to see them?"

"Not here. I'll have a look at them later. Who did he call?"

"Different people, and he placed a few of the calls himself so I didn't know who he was talking to. I think he made a few calls to Canada. He's sure somebody made a strike up there. Uranium or oil or gold or something, he doesn't know what it is but he's sure it's up there."

"He'll find out differently."

"I think he found out a little already. I managed to get him going when he was signing the letters I typed for him. He said he couldn't get any satisfaction, that nobody seemed to know a thing about a mineral strike in the area. And the date on your letter bothers him. He said he could see you coming down as a quick fast-buck operator if you'd heard about a strike, if you had advance information. But that letter is dated six or seven weeks ago, and if you had some information that long ago it would have spread by now. That's what has him hopping, the fact that nobody has heard a word about any developments in that section."

"That figures. Of course he hinted to me about uranium, and of course I said there was nothing like that, which was what he damn well expected me to say."

"He's just about ready to believe it now, John. And when I tell him what I managed to learn from you tonight, he'll be sure it's the straight story, or fairly close to it. How much of the play will I give him?"

"Not too much," I said. I lit a cigarette and drew on it. "Here's the steak," I said. "Let's forget the rest of this until later, all right? I want to give it time to settle."

We let it alone and worked on the steak. It was black on the outside and red in the middle, a nice match for the red leather and black wood decor of the room. I was hungrier than I'd realized. We made a little small talk, the usual routine about the food and the restaurant and the city itself. She wasn't too crazy about Olean. She didn't give me the chamber of commerce build-up I'd gotten earlier from her boss.

"I want to get out of here," she said. "You don't know what this town gets to be like. Like a prison cell."

I doubted it. I knew what a jail cell was like, and no town on earth was that way.

"You met Doug in Las Vegas?"

"That's right," she said. "I had a vacation and I just wanted to get away from all of this, and from Wally. I guess it was June when I went down there, the second or third week. I was supposed to go back, but I didn't plan on going back. His wife had been dead for eight months and he had just gotten around to telling me that he didn't plan on marrying me after all. It wouldn't look too good, he said, and what was the matter with things the way they stood?"

"What was?"

"Everything, as far as I was concerned. I was in a rut, John. A pretty deep one. I should have left this town a long while ago but I didn't have any place to go or anything much to do, and I figured I would stick with Wally and marry him when his wife died. He wasn't that exciting but he wasn't that bad and he does have money and, well, being poor is no pleasure."

"Agreed."

She managed a smile. "So by the time I found out I wasn't going to hear any wedding bells, I took this big long look at little Evelyn Stone and the neat little niche she had cut out for herself. I wasn't too taken with it, John. Here I'd spent a few years with a fairly romantic view of myself, the youngish girl with the wealthy older man, the office wife living a behind-the-scenes life. And then all at once I wasn't so young any more and I was just this girl Wallace J. Gunderman was keeping. And keeping damned cheaply. If you averaged it out, I was costing him less than if he bought it a shot at a time from a cheap streetwalker."

I didn't say anything. She studied her hands and said, "I don't like to say it that way, but about that time I started to see it that way, and it didn't sit well."

"Sure."

"So I went to Vegas for some fun and floor shows and roulette, and maybe a nice rich man would fall in love with me. Except I didn't like the men I met, and then too I couldn't afford the kind of vacation that might have put me in the right places at the right time. And I took a beating at the roulette wheel."

"And met Doug."

"Uh-huh." She smiled again. "He tried awfully hard to make me, but I just wasn't having any. I liked him, though. Right from the start I liked him."

"Everybody does."

"I suppose they must. After a while he must have decided that he wasn't going to wind up in bed with me, so he started talking to me and listening when I talked. He kept getting me to talk about Wally, and I did because I wanted to tell someone how mad I was at the son of a bitch. I didn't know what he was getting at. Then he came up with the idea and you know the rest of it."

I nodded. I liked the picture of Doug trying to score with her and striking out. It didn't exactly fit with the way he'd told it to me, but that figured. Nobody likes to paint pictures of himself in a foolish position.

"John? Did he say he slept with me?"

"No."

"The way you were smiling—"

"It's not that. He said that he didn't try, that he wasn't interested. And when I saw you in the office this morning I didn't get it."

"What do you mean?"

I met her eyes. "I couldn't imagine him not being interested. Not when I saw you."

"Oh," she said, and colored slightly. Then she said, "Listen, don't tell him what I said, will you? About him trying and not getting any place?"

"Don't worry."

"Because he might not like being reminded of it. But anyway, we got along fine once he quit being on the make. And he came up with this idea, and that changed my mind about coming back to Olean. I was back as soon as my vacation was up and went back to work for Wally."

I didn't ask the obvious question.

"Back to work in every respect," she said, answering the question I hadn't asked. "But it was different now. I don't feel like a cheap whore any more." The brown eyes flashed. "I feel like an expensive whore, John. A hundred-thousand-dollar call girl."

A busboy cleared our table. We passed up dessert and had coffee and cognac. The cognac was very old and very smooth. I broke out a fresh pack of cigarettes. She took one. I gave her a light and she leaned forward to take it. The jade heart fell away from her white skin. The black dress fell forward, too, and there was a momentary flash of the body beneath it, the thrust of breasts.

A hundred-thousand-dollar call girl. Our eyes locked and we smiled foolishly at each other.

The waiter brought the check. She added a tip and signed her name and, below that, Gunderman's. We got up and left.

Outside, it was cooler. She drove and I sat beside her. We didn't seem to be headed anywhere in particular.

She said, "This town. You'd think I'd be used to it by now, after six years here."

"Just six years? I thought you were born here."

"God, no." She pitched her cigarette out the window. "Not far from here, actually. I was brought up about twenty miles east of here, a little town called Bolivar. You probably never heard of it."

"I never even heard of Olean up to now."

"Then you never heard of Bolivar. It makes Olean look like New York. I got away from there to go to college. I went to Syracuse, to Syracuse University. I was on scholarship. I got married two weeks after graduation and wound up in New York."

"Doug told me you were married."

"I told him about it. When I start feeling sorry for myself I get carried away. I probably filled his ear with a lot of that. I married this boy from Long Island that I'd met at school and we went to New York to play house. I was the mommy and he was the man who took the suds out of the automatic washer. I don't know why I should be boring you with all this, John."

"I'm not bored."

"You're easy to talk to, aren't you?"

"Uh-huh. I used to be a psychiatrist before I turned crooked."

"I could almost believe that. What was I talking about?"

"The suds and the automatic washer."

"That's right. Except that we played it a little different. I was the mommy and he was the baby, that's what it all added up to, really. We never had enough money, either, and his parents hated me, really hated me, and then he started running around."

"That's hard to believe."

"You're nice, but he did. I didn't really feel insulted by it, to tell you the truth. I had managed to figure out by then that he was a nice boy but that I didn't want to spend the rest of my life with a nice boy who needed someone to wipe his nose and help him on with his rubbers. That came out dirty, I didn't mean it that way. You know what I meant."

"Uh-huh."

"So I went to Reno and threw my wedding ring in that river there, and came back to Bolivar, and there was a job opening in Olean, the job with Wally, and I took it, and you know the rest. I became a very private secretary. At first it was exciting and then it was secure and then his wife did die, finally, after hovering on the edge for years, and then we weren't going to get married after all and instead of a fiery affair it was a back-door thing with a bad smell to it."

Her fingers tightened on the steering wheel. When she spoke again her voice was thinner and higher. "I felt so goddamned good this afternoon. Watching that man, so hot to find a way to make a new fortune for himself, so excited he couldn't sit still. And knowing he's just going to get his nose rubbed in it, and that I'm going to do the rubbing. Oh, that's a sweet feeling!"

For a few minutes neither of us said anything. Her hands relaxed their grip on the wheel and she slowed the Ford and stopped at the curb. "There are things we ought to go over," she said. "You've got to tell me how much I'm supposed to tell him, for one thing, and then there are the letters he gave me. I've got them in my purse."

"Are we supposed to be making a night of it?"

"In a small way, anyway." Her eyes narrowed. "He didn't tell me how far to go playing the Mata Hari role. I guess I'm supposed to use my own imagination. There are bars we could go to, but they aren't all that private."

"My hotel room?"

"I thought of that. I think he might not like that. Everybody knows who I am, that I'm his secretary and that, well, that I'm more than his secretary. He might not like the way it would look if I went to your room."

"Where, then?"

"My apartment?"

"Fine."

"But I don't think I've got anything to drink."

We stopped for a bottle. I paid for it, and she insisted on giving me the money back when we got in the car. This was on Gunderman, she told me. He was footing the bill for the evening.

Six

She lived in a newish brick apartment building on Irving Street. Her place was on the second floor. She tucked the Ford into a parking space out in front and we walked up a flight of stairs. She unlocked the door and we went inside. The living room was large and airy, furnished in Danish Modern pieces that looked expensive. The carpet was deep and ran wall-to-wall. It wasn't hard to guess who paid the rent, or who had picked up the tab for the furnishings.

"I'll hunt glasses," she said. "How do you like your poison? Water, soda?"

"Just rocks is fine."

She came back from the kitchen with a pair of drinks. We sat together on a long low couch and touched glasses solemnly. "Here's to crime," she said.

"To successful crime."

"By all means."

We drank. She tucked her feet under her, opened her purse and pulled out a sheaf of letters. "He had a list of people who bought some of that Canadian land," she said. "Not a complete list, but about twenty names. He wrote letters to all of them asking—well, you can read it yourself."

I read one of the letters. It was brief and to the point. Mr. Gunderman was interested in any dealings or correspondence that Mr. So-and-So might have had with the Barnstable Corporation, Ltd., of Toronto. Would Mr. So-and-So please let Mr. Gunderman know, and would he also notify Mr. Gunderman if he had made any disposition of his holdings in north-western Canada, or if he had any intention of so doing?

There were eighteen letters like that. Gunderman's list didn't match ours completely. He was missing a lot of the names we'd gotten from Al Prince, and he had one or two that Prince hadn't given to us. I picked out the letters to the ten men with whom we'd been in correspondence and handed them back to Evvie.

"You can mail these," I told her. "They'll tell him just what we want him to know. A few of these pigeons already sold land to us, and the rest have heard from us."

"What about the others?"

"I'll keep them."

"Won't he get suspicious if he doesn't hear anything from any of those men?"

"He'll hear from them. What other letters did he dictate?"

I looked through them. There was a letter to the Ontario Board of Trade inquiring in a general way into the commercial purpose and history of Barnstable, and there was a very similar letter addressed to the Lieutenant-General's office. I let those go through.

Both of those sources would simply advise Gunderman that we had incorporated at such-and-such a date with so much capital, and that we had organized for the purpose of purchasing and developing land in the western provinces.

This was all a matter of public record, and it was something we wanted Gunderman to know. We could tell him ourselves, but it was much better to let him find out on his own hook from properly official government sources. Let him think he was being shrewd. If you let a man convince himself that he is much cleverer than you are, he will never get around to fearing that you're going to pull a fast one on him.

"And this one here," she said.

The last letter was addressed to a Toronto detective agency that specialized in industrial and financial investigations. Gunderman asked for a brief report on (a) the Barnstable Corporation, Ltd., (b) Douglas Rance, and (c) John Hayden.

"He asked me to put a call through to these people," Evvie said. "I told him I couldn't get through to them and I killed the call, and then he put it all in a letter. I was a little afraid of what might come out. I know he used this agency before, when he got taken the first time."

"I don't think this letter should go out."

"That's what I figured. And why I cut off the call. If a detective dug into things too deeply—"

"Uh-huh."

"But if he doesn't hear from them at all—"

"He'll hear from them," I said. I swallowed some Scotch, got a cigarette going. She pursed her lips, moistened them with the tip of her tongue. She started to say something, then changed her mind and finished her drink. I went into the kitchen, filled a bowl with ice cubes, brought it and the bottle back into the living room. I put the bowl on the coffee table and added fresh ice and fresh Scotch to our glasses.

"What should we drink to this time, John?"

"*Salud y amor y pesetas,*" I said.

"Health and love and money, I know that one. Isn't there more to it?"

"*Y tiempo para gustarlos.*"

"And time...what's the rest of it?"

"And time to enjoy them."

"And time to enjoy them," she said. "Yes, that's worth drinking to."

We touched glasses very solemnly and drank a toast to health and love and money and time to enjoy them. Outside, Olean remained very peaceful by night. The few traffic noises were all blocks away. I looked at her and felt that old urge come on strong from out of nowhere, a fast rush of desire that surprised me. A comfortable couch, a quiet and properly private apartment, a good bottle, a beautiful girl—all of them components in a standard mixture. I put a lid on it and started to tell her just what she should say to Gunderman in the morning.

I ran all the way through it. It was simple enough, no details but a few hints to steer him in the right direction. The hunting lodge story was a blind, of course. I'd been hopping all over the country lately, and I had bought up a great deal of land, and the Barnstable Corporation stood to make a fortune. I was just a hired hand, and I was a little resentful of the fact that I was on straight salary, albeit a healthy salary, while the principals in the deal stood to pick up a bundle without doing much work for it at all. Of course they were very important men and I was just an employee, so I really had no kick coming. Barnstable already owned a vast stretch of Canadian land, and few prospects had given me a hard time the way Gunderman had done, and I didn't care too much whether I bought his land or not, because we already had done so well in the land-purchasing department.

When I got to the end I let her feed it all back to me. She didn't miss a trick, and she added a touch or two all her own. She was very damned good for an amateur. She had the brains for it, and the right attitude. She was a natural girl for the grift. If this fell in, I thought, or even if it didn't, she could probably make a damned fine living as the female half of a badger game combo. She sure as hell had the looks for it.

She filled our glasses again. She said, "You know, I was very nervous about all of this before tonight, John. I'm not nervous any more."

"What changed your mind?"

"You did."

"Me?"

She nodded. "Uh-huh. Doug was all fire and enthusiasm and confidence, but I wasn't sure he could bring it all off. But there's something about you, I don't know what it is, maybe just a feeling that you really know what you're doing, that you'll make sure everything runs smoothly from start to finish." Her eyes narrowed slightly. "I somehow just trust you, John."

"Let's hope your boss feels the same way."

"I think he will. I'm awfully glad Doug was able to get you in on this deal. He told me about you when we were first starting to plan the whole thing, and he said you would be perfect if only you weren't working on something else. That's what I was afraid of, that you would have something else going."

"I did."

"Oh?"

"I was assistant manager at a bowling alley in Colorado."

"Really?"

"Really."

"I don't—"

I drank some more. "I got out of prison a little less than a year ago, Evvie. It was the first really hard time I'd ever served, and I decided I wasn't going back, not ever. I took a square job and stuck with it." I put my glass down. "Then Doug Rance turned up with a proposition. I said no to him a few times and wound up saying yes."

"What changed your mind?"

Sometimes you have to share your dreams. It was the Scotch or the girl or a combination of the two, I suppose. I told her about Bannion's dump outside of Boulder and how it would pay off like a broken slot machine with the right sort of operation. And how I couldn't go there for a drink without itching for the money to buy the place and run it the way it ought to be run. And how I was in this deal for the money because there was no other way for me to get that money, and when the deal was done I would be back in Boulder, through with the grift forever and all set to make decent money on the square.

She asked a few questions and I answered them. Then we were both a long time silent. Our glasses were empty. I let them stay that way. I had enough of a load to feel it and I didn't want to get drunk. We smoked a few cigarettes. I kept trying not to look at her, and kept failing in the attempt. This was dangerous. The more I looked at her the more I came up with crazy images. Pictures of the two of us on top of a Colorado mountain, walking hand in hand, as fresh and breathlessly natural as a commercial for mentholated cigarettes. The American Dream, stock footage number 40938.

Well, we all of us had our weaknesses. Doug gambled, I fell in love. It was nothing I wouldn't be able to put a lid on. But I didn't want any more to drink, not now.

"John."

I turned to her.

"I hope you get what you want, John."

We looked at each other. She was curled up on that couch beside me like a large cat in front of a fireplace.

I knew what I wanted. I wanted to make her purr.

"John—"

I reached for her; she came to me. She smelled as clean and alive as a newly mowed lawn. I kissed her, and she went rigid and made a weird little sound deep in her throat, and then her arms were tight around me and the tension was gone and we kissed again.

We broke. I lit two cigarettes and gave one of them to her. Her hand was trembling. She dropped the cigarette, and I got down on my hands and knees and chased it. It had bounced under the couch. I picked it up and rubbed the spot where the carpet was lightly scorched. She took it from me and drew on it, coughed, crushed it out in the ashtray. She straightened up and closed her eyes tight. Her hands bunched up into nervous little fists.

"I didn't want this to happen, John."

I said nothing.

"I don't, I can't, I—"

I waited.

"It has to be real. I don't want another…I can't…it has to mean something. It has to—"

I stood up. She hesitated, then got to her feet. I kissed her and held her close. Her body pressed against me all the way. I kissed her again and crushed her closer.

"Yes," she said.

Afterward she lay on her side with her eyes closed and a lazy grin on her lips. She made a sweet purring sound. I got out of her bed and padded into the living room. The ice had melted. I got fresh ice from the refrigerator and made stiff drinks for both of us. I brought the drinks and our cigarettes back to the bedroom. She had not changed position. She still lay on her side, the same sweet ghost of a smile on her lips. She was still purring.

I put the drinks and the cigarettes on the bedside table and kissed her.

"Mmmmm," she said. She opened her eyes and yawned luxuriously. "Oh, God," she said. "I really didn't want this to happen."

"Neither did I."

"But I'm glad it did. What time is it?"

"Almost one."

"Is it that late already? I thought it was about ten o'clock."

"That was three hours ago."

"Maybe you'd better get dressed."

"I guess so."

"I wish you could sleep here, but I think you should probably sleep at your hotel. I don't want Wally to know about this. Actions above and beyond the call of duty. He might even approve, goddamn him. But I don't want him to know about it, or Doug Rance either."

"Don't worry."

She had a special beauty nude. Most women look better clothed. Bodies are imperfect. Clothes hide, and also promise, and the promise is too often better than the fulfillment of it. Not so with Evvie.

She still wore the jade heart. I touched it, let my fingers trail down to her breasts. She purred again.

"I'll get dressed and drive you back."

"Don't be silly."

"Well, you can't walk, for God's sake."

"Why not? It's a nice night."

"It's a long walk."

"How far?"

"Nine or ten blocks, I think. All the way down to North Union and then over to the hotel. Let me drive you, John."

"I feel like walking."

I dressed. I finished my drink and she worked on hers. It was late and the night outside was cold and quiet.

I said, "He's going to keep you busy tomorrow morning with a million crazy questions. You know what to tell him. Then he may want to see me, or he may try to stall for more time. I don't think I should let him stall too much. I'm going to grab a plane tomorrow afternoon."

"For Toronto?"

"Yes." I drew on a cigarette. "The more I think about it, the more I think I shouldn't see him tomorrow. It would be good if he got tied up with something during the morning that kept him busy until two or three in the afternoon, and then by the time he was ready for me it would be too late and I would have already left for the airport. I think that's the way to do it, to give him the rope so that he can rope himself in a little."

"What do you have to do in Toronto?"

"A lot of things. I'll dodge around for about a week to give him time to get answers to his letters. Keep a close watch on him in the meantime. If he starts to go off the track, don't keep it a secret. Get on the goddamn phone and call us."

"Where?"

"You have the Barnstable number. It's on our letterhead. Just call and talk to Doug."

"Suppose I want to talk to you?"

I told her what hotel I was staying at, and how to reach me. I didn't spend too much time at the hotel. I told her to leave messages if I wasn't there, to give her name as Miss Carmody. If there was a message to the effect that Miss Carmody had called, I would try her first at her apartment and then at the office.

"And when will I see you again, John?"

"In about a week, maybe ten days. I think he'll probably try to get in touch with us, and we'll give him a short stall and then make contact again, probably with me coming down here to Olean again."

She didn't say anything. I knotted my tie and made the knot properly small and neat. I put a foot on a chair and tied my shoe. I stubbed out my cigarette in the ashtray on the bedside table. It was a copper-enameled ashtray with a red and green geometric design on it, the sort of thing women make in Golden-Ager classes at the YWCA.

She said, "I'll miss you."

"Evvie—"

She stood up. I turned to her and kissed her. She was all breathless and shaky. There were deep circles under her eyes.

"I hope I'm not just part of the game, John. Cheat the mooch and sleep with the girl, all of it part of a package deal. I hope—"

"You know better."

"I hope so," she said.

The air was cool, the sky clear. There was a nearly full moon and a scattering of stars. Irving Street was wide, with tall shade trees lining the curbs on both sides of the street. The houses were set back a good ways from the curb. They were single homes built forty or fifty years ago. Most of them had upstairs porches. Some had bay windows and other gingerbread. I walked eight blocks down Irving to North Union without meeting anyone. A single car passed me, a cab, empty. He slowed, I shook my head, and he went on.

All but a few of the houses were completely dark inside. Here and there a light would be on upstairs, and in two houses I could see television screens flickering in darkened living rooms.

I turned left at North Union, crossed the street, found my way back to the Olean House. The lobby was deserted except for a sleepy old man at the desk and a very old woman who sat in one of the chairs opposite the fireplace reading a newspaper. I picked up my key at the desk and took the elevator upstairs.

It happens more often than it doesn't. You're

caught up in something fast-moving and exciting and secretive, and this sudden common bond masks all of the things that you do not have in common, and moments are infused with a deceptive sort of vitality, and you wind up in the rack. Bells ring, all of that.

I went over to my window. There was nothing in particular to look at. Most of the stores on the main drag didn't even bother keeping their windows lit. I smoked a cigarette.

It happens all the time. You try not to let it get mixed that way, the business and the pleasure. Like not going where you eat, a similar attempt to separate disparate functions. It is rarely as easy as it sounds, and circumstances can make it harder.

I was an old buck gone long in the tooth with an age-old weakness for pretty girls. And she had had four years of Wallace J. Gunderman, and simple biology could make her ready enough for a change of pace, especially when she could so easily talk herself into thinking that it all meant something. So it was all something to take and enjoy and forget soon after. It was just what she had said she hoped it wasn't—part of the fruits of the game, her body along with her boss's money. Take it and enjoy it and kiss it good-bye.

I got undressed and hung everything up neatly. I stood under a too-hot shower. I got out of the shower and sat on the edge of the bed and smoked another cigarette.

I told myself not to think about it. I put out my cigarette and reached for the phone. It took the old man a long time to answer. I gave him my name and my room number and told him to ring me at eleven, and not to put any calls through before then. He asked me to wait a minute. He dug up a pencil and I repeated the instructions to him very slowly while he wrote everything down. Then he read it back to me and I said yes indeed, fine, perfect.

I cradled the phone. I thought about the color of the jade heart against her white skin, and her eyes and hair and the way she smelled and the small sounds she made.

I went to bed and to sleep.

Seven

I'd been up for an hour and a half when the phone rang at eleven. The woman said, "It's eleven o'clock, Mr. Hayden. You had several phone calls, but I didn't put them through because there was a message that you weren't to be disturbed."

"Fine. Any messages?"

"The calls were all from Mr. Gunderman," she said. She made the name sound almost holy. "You're to call him as soon as possible."

I sat around the hotel room for another half hour. I packed my suitcase, smoked a few cigarettes. I left the suitcase by the side of the bed and went downstairs for breakfast. At noon I called Gunderman's office from a pay phone across the street.

Evvie answered. "I'm sorry, Mr. Hayden," she said. "Mr. Gunderman is out to lunch."

"I'm at a pay phone," I said. "You can talk."

"He'll be sorry he missed your call, Mr. Hayden. He's been trying to reach you all morning, but he had a luncheon appointment and he was called out."

"Oh, I get it. There's someone in the office."

"That's quite correct, Mr. Hayden."

"Who is it? Gunderman?"

"No, I don't believe so."

"All right, it doesn't matter. I'll give you questions you can answer without any trouble. When do you expect him back?"

"Perhaps an hour, Mr. Hayden."

"How did he take the line you handed him? Was he with it all the way?"

"Yes, that's right."

"And he's very anxious to see me?"

"I believe so, yes."

"Then I think it's just as well that he doesn't. There's a plane leaving Ischua Airport at four-thirty this afternoon. When he comes in, tell him I was over to the office. Can you do that?"

"Yes."

"And that I was sorry we couldn't get together, but I had a few things hanging fire that I had to take care of, and that I'd try to get in touch with him in a week or so. Give him the general impression that I'm sorry I wasted my time here but if he wants to sell and take his tax loss the offer is still open. I'm not pushing, but I'm willing. Have you got that?"

"Yes."

"I wish I could stay another day. I'll get back as soon as I can, Evvie. There's no chance of you getting up to Toronto for a day, is there?"

"No, I don't believe so."

"Uh-huh. You might get him to send you on a reconnaissance mission, but that's probably not that good an idea. I'll miss you."

Silence.

"Bye, baby."

I cradled the phone. I picked up a paperback and a couple of magazines and went back to the hotel. I sat around in the room for an hour while Gunderman ate his lunch, then checked out of the hotel and caught a cab to the airport. I got there better than three hours before flight time. I checked my bag and walked down the road a little ways to a tavern. I nursed a few drinks and listened to a juke box. The place was very nearly empty.

At four-thirty my plane left, and I was on it.

Doug had to hear all of it twice through. He made a perfect audience. He hung on every word and grinned at every clever turn of phrase and nodded approvingly at every halfway cute gambit. I kept expecting him to burst into spontaneous applause.

"You roped him," he said admiringly. "You lassoed that son of a bitch."

"He's not branded yet."

"Now we stick it in and break it off, Johnny. Jesus, this is beautiful. How long do you want to leave him hanging? A week?"

"More or less."

"Won't he try to reach us before then?"

"He won't be able to reach me. If he calls Barnstable, they'll tell him I'm out. The girl will. The girl doesn't even know me, does she?"

"She's met you. I don't know if she remembers the name."

"She didn't meet me as Claude Whittlief, did she?"

"No."

"Because if she did, we'd have to get rid of her before the payoff. No, I'm sure she didn't, now that I think about it. So if he tries to reach me he won't get any place, and I don't think he'd want to go over my head and talk with you. If he's as shrewd as I figure him to be, he'll want to work through me, to use me to get the inside dope and to make whatever pitch he might want to make. Remember, he only has a little bit of the picture now, only as much as Evvie's given him."

"How did you like her, incidentally?"

"She's all right."

"Get anywheres?"

"I didn't try," I said.

"Not interested?"

"Not on a job."

His grin spread. "That's the professional attitude, all right. I could go another cup of coffee. You?"

"Fine."

We were in a booth at an all-night diner on Dundas about a block or so from my hotel. The food was greasy and so were most of the customers. The coffee wasn't too bad. A bucktoothed waitress with a West Virginia accent brought us more of it. She was a long way from home.

"About those letters," he said. "How do you want to handle them?"

I had gone over the letters Gunderman had written to those other pigeons. Of the eighteen, ten had been to people we were already in correspondence with, and those Evvie had mailed. I had the other eight. One man lived in Buffalo, two in Cleveland, one in Toledo, one in a Chicago suburb, two in New York City, and one way the hell up in Seattle.

"We throw out the Seattle one, first of all," I said. "It won't hurt him if he doesn't get a reply from everybody, and Seattle is too damn far to run to just to get a postmark."

"There are remailing services," he suggested.

I sipped coffee, put the cup down. "The hell with those. I ran one of those myself about twelve years back. *Letters Re-mailed—25¢. Your Secret Address. Mail Forwarded and Received.* I opened every letter and sold the interesting ones to a blackmailer. Somehow I don't think I was the only grifter to run one of those outfits."

"That's one racket I never heard of."

"Everything's a racket," I said. "The day after tomorrow, I'll have the letters ready. I'll spend tomorrow taking care of the stationery angle. Then I'll fly to Chicago and mail a letter and work my way back on the trains. The cities spread out in a line, Chicago and Toledo and Cleveland and Buffalo, and then a plane down to New York and back again. That's no problem."

"And the detective agency?"

That was a problem, all right. If we didn't answer that letter at all, Gunderman would get on the phone and call them himself. Evvie couldn't head off the calls

forever. If we *did* answer, using a fake sheet of the
firm's letterhead (or even a real sheet; it wouldn't be
all that hard to run up to their offices and filch a piece
of paper and an envelope) we would run into head-
winds when Gunderman called to thank them, or sent
along a check in payment.

"Let it lie for a day or two," Doug suggested. "He
won't expect a report from them by return mail,
anyway. We'll think of something."

In the morning I got busy on the handful of letters.
There was a printer in town who specialized in doing a
little work on the wrong side of the law. He did job-
printing for the boys who printed up pornography and
trucked it across the bridge into the States, and he was
supposed to be fairly good at passports and other doc-
uments. I could have had him run off a few different
batches of stationery for us, but I didn't want to.

We already had a use for him—he was going to
draw up the fake deeds for us, deeds to Canadian land
which we did not own. I've never been very tall on the
idea of using the same person too many times in a
single job. It's not a good idea to let one man get that
much of a picture of your operation. He would handle
the deeds, and do a good job with that, and that was
enough.

I went to a batch of printers and a couple of office
supply stores. Each printer made up a batch of a hundred sheets and envelopes, and the stationery stores
came through with cheaper standard stuff. I had seven

letters to answer, and I wound up with seven hundred sheets and envelopes, each batch with a different name and address and city, each on different paper and in different ink. I got one-day service from everybody, and by six o'clock that evening I had everything I needed.

We typed out four of the responses and wrote out three by hand. We used the office typewriter, cleaning the keys after the first letter, knocking a letter out of alignment before the third one, and otherwise disguising the fact that all four letters were coming out of the same machine. The handwritten letters were no problem at all. I have five very different styles of handwriting, and Doug has about as many. An expert could find enough similarities to guess that any of my five styles was my writing, but the average person would never see a connection. And Gunderman would not be putting our letters under a microscope. The pens were different, the inks different, the envelopes would be zooming in from different cities—he wasn't going to run to a handwriting expert as an extra safeguard.

We varied the text of the letters, too. Five of our seven men wrote Gunderman to tell him that they had sold their land to Barnstable, that Barnstable had paid off promptly and legitimately, and would Gunderman tell them what was the matter with the operation? (I guessed that he wouldn't answer, not wanting to get people curious. If he did, Evvie could simply throw the letters away.) One man replied that he used his land for summer camping and was not interested in selling it to Barnstable, to Gunderman, or to anybody else. The last man, the one in Toledo, wrote that he had turned down Barnstable's first offer in the hope that they might raise it, and that so far they hadn't.

Doug and I both worked on the wording. We kept the letters short and to the point. By the time we were through, the letters were set to do their job. They would convey the impression we were aiming at. Our man Gunderman would be left with the impression that the Barnstable Corporation, Ltd., had managed to buy up half of Canada for a song. Our man Gunderman would be starting to drool.

"The detective agency," he said. "Any ideas?"

"None that I'm too crazy about. It would be easy if they had never done any work for Gunderman before. I could go to them, introduce myself as Gunderman, and give them some very minor piece of work to do for me. Then in the meantime I send Gunderman a faked report on a copy of their letterhead, along with a bill for the same amount as their bill to me. His check would go to them and it would cover the work I'd done, and that would touch all the bases neatly enough." I shrugged. "But they've worked for him, and that queers it. They might know him, or at least know enough to know I wasn't Wallace J. Gunderman. And besides, I don't like the idea that much to begin with."

"It's a little shaky."

"Uh-huh."

He looked at me. "Maybe we should let the letter go through."

"I don't like that, either."

"What can they find out about us that isn't legit?"

"You'd be surprised."

He thought that over and decided he agreed with me. "We'll work it out," he assured me. "You get those letters in the mail and I'll see if I can't come up with something."

"Sure. I might be two or three days."

"Take your time."

"Right."

"And don't get hung up on the detective angle. We'll think of something good."

"Sure."

I called Evvie's apartment that night. I let the phone ring a dozen times before I gave up, and I called back half an hour later and let it ring another dozen times without getting an answer. It was around midnight by then and she wasn't home, and I knew she must be with Gunderman and I tried not to let it bother me. What the hell, she had warmed his bed for four years already. I couldn't exactly turn jealous because she was playing the same role.

Besides, it was part of the game, wasn't it? It happened all the time. A good percentage of the long cons had a sex angle, with a girl's body helping to tie the mark up tight. The one that put me in San Quentin was one like that. Our mooch started sleeping with a girl who told him she was pregnant. I'd been sleeping with that girl myself, and not in a completely casual way. I hadn't liked it when she spent too much time around other men. But it didn't rub me the wrong way when she played with the mooch. That was part of the game, part of setting him up for the score.

I worked that job as roper. I was the mooch's friend, helping set up the phony abortion. I remembered how I sat with him in the waiting room, how he bit his nails and how his sweat smelled, cold and rancid. And the "doctor"—Sweet Raymond Conn, dead of a heart attack while awaiting trial—the doctor coming out to the waiting room with horrible eyes to tell us that something had gone wrong, that our little girl was dead as a lox.

Instead of operating, Conn had worked on the girl with makeup. He led the mooch inside, I followed, and Peggy was all spread out on a long white table with waxy cheeks and pale flesh and dead staring eyes. I was terrified that she would blink. She didn't, and not six hours later she scrubbed off the deadish makeup and I took her to bed.

I hadn't seen her since the trial. She drew one-to-five, no previous record and her lawyer did a good job for her, and she was on the street within six months. God knows where she is now, or what she's doing.

So I had no reason to sweat because Evvie was busy earning her keep. Anyway, I didn't own her. One roll in the rack, one sweet time that sealed a bargain and made the gears mesh more perfectly, that was all it was. No burning passion, no eternal flame of love.

◦

I flew to Chicago in the morning with no luggage but a briefcase with a batch of letters in it. The cab from O'Hare Airport to the downtown train station happened to pass through the suburb where Gunderman's unwitting correspondent hung his hat. It was a coincidence worth taking advantage of. I made the hackie stop while I dropped the letter in a mailbox, then rode on to the train station.

The Central had a train that went to New York by way of Toledo, Ashtabula, Cleveland, and Albany. It left around eleven-thirty in the morning. We had enough of a stopover at Toledo for me to duck into the terminal and drop the letter in a mailbox and get back to the train on time. In Cleveland, I left the train and had dinner at a downtown restaurant and mailed another two letters. The next train that went on to Buffalo made too many stops. I passed it up and caught another an hour and a half later, mailed my Buffalo letter and took a ride out to the airport.

There were no more planes that night, by the time I got there. I took a room at a motel across from the airport and left an early morning call. I got up, showered, and called Toronto. Nothing was new, Doug told me. I made my plane and was at La Guardia an hour and twenty minutes later. I took the limousine into Manhattan, mailed the last two letters, rode back to the airport and caught a luncheon flight for Toronto by way of Montreal.

All of this was a lot of travel with not much to do. Detail work, moronically simple, automatic, and fairly expensive. I believe in details. They are almost always worth the trouble.

We had bought seven hundred sheets and envelopes of stationery, used seven, and thrown away the other six hundred ninety-three. All this to keep a crooked printer from figuring out too much of our angle. I had trained and planed around two thousand miles because I didn't believe in remail services, and because there was a bare possibility that Gunderman noticed postmarks on his mail. I didn't regret a dollar of the expense or a minute of the time invested. When you're pulling the string on a big one, you want the whole superstructure to be just right.

I took my time dropping over to the Barnstable office. When I got there it was past five and our secretary was gone for the day. Doug was sitting at his desk looking busy.

"Everything done?"

"Done and done," I said.

He got a bottle from his desk and made drinks for us. "Your friend in Olean is starting to get warm," he told me. "Three calls for you today, one in the morning and two this afternoon. I had the girl tell him you were out of town the last time he called. Before that she just said you weren't in."

"Good."

"You were right on one thing, incidentally. He didn't ask to talk to me. And he didn't really want to give his name to the girl, either. He did, but he was reluctant about it."

I nodded.

"So everything's moving, Johnny."

"Except for the detective agency."

"I've got an angle on that, Johnny."

"What is it?"

"Watch," he said. He looked very pleased with himself. He picked up the phone and dialed the operator. He told her he wanted to place a person-to-person call for Mr. Wallace J. Gunderman in Olean, New York. He gave her Gunderman's office number.

"You can't talk to him," I said.

"I can. You can't, because he knows you. He hasn't talked to me yet, and by the time he meets me he'll have forgotten my voice."

"But—"

He held up a hand. He said, "Mr. Gunderman? This is Gerald Morphy, of Brennan Scientific Investigations. You wrote us about an outfit called the Barnstable Corporation?" A pause. "Mr. Gunderman, I wanted to tell you right away that I don't believe we'll be able to handle this investigation ourselves. Right at the moment we've got almost all of our operatives tied up on an industrial sabotage thing, and we're not accepting any other cases at the moment."

Another pause. Then, "I do have a suggestion. If it's satisfactory to you, I'd like to refer the matter to another investigator, a man named Robert Hettinger. He's worked for us in the past. He has his own office now and he's quite reliable and honest. Would that...yes, certainly. Yes, he'd make his reports directly to you and you could make your own financial arrangements with him. This looks to be a small matter, Mr. Gunderman, and while I wish we could serve you directly…yes, well, I can guarantee the man's work personally. Yes, fine, Mr. Gunderman, and it's my pleasure, sir."

He put the phone down and smiled across the desk at me. He looked as triumphant as a sparring partner who'd just knocked out Liston. "In two or three days," he said, "we send him this."

He handed me a two-page letter. The letterhead read *Robert M. Hettinger…private investigative service…404 Richmond West…Toronto*. The report said everything we could have wanted it to say. It invented a fine upstanding background for Rance, who was cast as a scion of an established Toronto family with a background in shipping and land development. It said that I was new in Toronto, an employee of Barnstable, and so on. We couldn't have worked up a cleaner bill of health for ourselves.

There was also a bill for fifty dollars Canadian for services rendered.

I said, "Who's Hettinger?"

"I am."

"And the address?"

"You can rent office space at four-o-four Richmond for five dollars a month. I get a desk and mail privileges for that much. I paid them five dollars, and they'll have Gunderman's check for me when he sends it along." He grinned elaborately. "Fifty dollars, and when you subtract the cost of the stationery and the phone call and the month's rent on the desk space, we still come out about twenty dollars ahead. I figured we might as well pick up pin money along the way."

"And if he tries to call you?"

"There's a girl who answers the phone for everybody on the floor there. If he calls, Mr. Hettinger is out. But he won't. He'll get the report and send a check, and that's all."

It was neat and I told him so. He was as hungry for praise as a puppy who had finally succeeded in getting the puddle on the paper. He poured more Scotch for us and as we drank to success, I told him again how neatly he'd fielded the ball, and that was that.

I called Evvie from my hotel. This time she was home. I said, "John here. You alone, baby?"

"Yes. What is it?"

"Just a progress report. Everything's running smoothly on this end. Your boss is going to start getting letters any day now."

"Good."

I told her about the detective agency routine. She thought it was very clever, and I didn't bother mentioning that it was Doug's idea. I asked her how Gunderman was behaving.

"He's falling all the way," she said.

"I understand he's trying to reach me."

"Three times today, John. He was upset when you managed to leave town the other day without seeing him. He's positive there's something going on that he could make money on. He doesn't know what the gimmick is but he's sure there is one and he's dying to find it. How much longer do you want to let him dangle?"

I thought about it. "Maybe I'll take another trip to Olean soon," I said.

"That would be nice."

"Let's see. I think maybe the middle of the week, maybe on Wednesday. He should have enough replies by Monday afternoon so that the whole picture will soak in fast enough. Now here's the bit. Monday, you'll tell him that you got a call from me. I wasn't in Toronto, you're not sure where I was, but I wasn't in Toronto. I called you, and it seems as though I'm anxious to see you, not Gunderman but you. You have the feeling that I'm halfway crazy about you, and—"

"Are you, John?"

"What?"

"Halfway crazy about me?"

I lit a cigarette. "Anyway, at this point you became the little heroine, doing it up right for the boss. You knew he wanted to see me, so you conned me into coming down to Olean on the excuse of seeing Gunderman. He'll be delighted. And set it up so that I'll come around to his office sometime Wednesday afternoon."

"You didn't answer my question, John."

"Did you get what I said?"

"Of course. You still didn't answer my question."

"I'll give you the answer in person," I said.

I wound up sitting at the bar at The Friars. They had a piano trio there that wasn't half bad, a West Coast outfit a long way from home. The bass player had worked with Mulligan ages ago. I stayed there until the place closed and walked back to my hotel.

Eight

"Have a seat, John," he said. "Just have a seat and relax. You must have had quite a trip. I hate those little puddle-hopping airlines. You no sooner get your belt fastened than it's time to unhook it because you've landed already; just up and down again. And I guess you've had a belly full of travel lately, haven't you?"

"Well, I've been busy."

"Now I'm sure you have, John. I'm sure you have at that. I wish I hadn't missed you that morning. Your hotel wouldn't put an early call through to your room, and then you were gone before I could get hold of you. I was sorry about that."

"I meant to come over in the morning," I said. "But it turned out, well, to be quite a late night, and then I went and did more drinking than I usually do, and I felt I ought to sleep a little later than usual. And then when I did wake up—"

I left the sentence hanging. Gunderman nodded slowly and said, "I suppose you weren't feeling too well, John."

"No, I guess I wasn't."

"Probably a little bit of a hangover?"

"Well, I felt a little rocky."

"I can imagine. I guess Evvie did a good job of showing you the town. I wish I could have come myself. Still, she's better at playing host than I am. And a damn sight better looking than I am, as far as that goes. I think she's taken a shine to you, John."

I did a good job of trying not to look embarrassed. I took a cigarette and fumbled for matches. He gave me a light and relit his cigar. He could see that I was ill at ease and nothing could have delighted him more. He was enjoying himself tremendously.

"You're a hard man to get hold of, John," he said. "I couldn't get your home telephone number, so I had to try you at your office. I'm afraid I made quite a few calls. They didn't tell me that you were out of town at first, just that you weren't in and they didn't know where you could be reached. Then they did tell me you were out of town, but didn't seem to know when you'd be back, so I just went on calling. Your bosses must really keep you hopping."

"I did a lot of traveling this trip," I admitted.

"Get much accomplished?"

"Well," I said vaguely.

"Buy a lot of land, John?"

I coughed on my cigarette. I looked at him nervously, and he looked back and let his eyebrows climb up a notch. I met his eyes and drew again on my cigarette. I didn't say anything, but then I didn't have to. We had reached a quiet understanding. I was telling him that I knew that he knew that our hunting lodge story was a lot of hooey, but that I wasn't too crazy about the idea of discussing it, not for now, anyway.

"Well," he said easily. "I ought to tell you, John, that I've had time to think over your proposition, and while the tax-loss features are attractive, certainly, I'm afraid I'm not interested in selling my property. Not for the time being, at least."

"I see."

"You don't seem very disappointed."

I leaned forward in my chair, stubbed out my cigarette in his ashtray, and narrowed my eyes. I said, "I'm afraid I had more to drink the other night than I usually do. When I was out with Ev—with your secretary. I guess I talked a little more than I wanted to, and I guess she relayed some of what I said to you."

He just smiled.

"The men who employ me trust me to do my job, Wally, and part of doing my job is keeping certain matters confidential. I…if I said anything that I shouldn't have said, and if it got back to you, well, I just wish you'd forget it."

"Oh? You don't have to worry about my making trouble for you, John."

"It's not that, but—"

"And if it'll set your mind at rest, you didn't tell me so very much through Evvie. Or if you did tell her everything, then she held out on me." He chuckled to let me know how plainly impossible it was that she might keep anything from him. "But I do know a lot more about the operations of the Barnstable outfit than I ever learned from you. After all, I wouldn't keep calling you in Toronto just to tell you that I wasn't interested in your proposition, would I?"

"I didn't think so, no."

"Hardly. Would you like to know what I've managed to learn?"

I nodded, and he told me. He parroted back just about every fact we had arranged for him to uncover. He gave me dates and figures and names and I let my jaw drop progressively as he built himself up a good head of steam. When he finished I just sat there shaking my head.

"I couldn't have let all of that slip to Evvie."

"You didn't, John."

"Why, there are things you know that I don't even know, like exactly when the company was organized. How did you—"

He waved all of this away with one hand. "When you've been in business as long as I have," he said, "you know how to get information. And you'd be surprised how easy it is to find something out once you've made up your mind. When someone comes to offer me money, John, I want to know something about him. When someone wants to buy something from me, I like to know what it is he plans to do with it." He set the cigar aside and folded his hands on the desk top. "And that still has me up in the air. You people have bought all of that land, and by God, you've put your hands on a hell of a lot of land. How much acreage would you say you've got, John?"

"I don't honestly know," I said.

"Oh?"

"I've seen quite a few people, but a large portion of our dealings have been carried on through the mails, or over the telephone. I'm only sent on the road when we don't get anywhere through the mail. So I honestly don't know how large the corporate holdings are, Wally."

"But Barnstable owns quite a bit of land, wouldn't you say?"

"Oh, of course."

"Now that's as far as I can go with it," he said. He sat back and scratched his head. "I'll tell you the truth, John, I'm damned if I can figure out what you people plan to do with that land. Now I can see that you've been very clever about this. Not you personally, John, but your company, in hitting on this method of purchasing land. By dealing with people who've been cheated on this land in the first place, you're putting yourselves in a position where you can steal it right back."

"Not steal it," I said. "We—"

"Figure of speech, John, but let's not mince words. You folks are picking up that land at a hell of a lot less than it's worth. When you offered me five hundred dollars for land I sank twenty thousand into, all I could see was the difference between five hundred and twenty thousand. Which is a hell of a difference. And I'm damn certain that's all anybody sees when they come up against your offer. When a man overpays for a piece of property the way I overpaid for that stretch of goddamned moose pasture, all he can see is that he got taken, that he laid out money for something worthless.

"But that land's not worthless because, damn it, no land is worthless, no matter where it is. I ought to know that if anybody should. Hell, the land I've bought that people said wasn't worth a damn, and the money I made on it while those jokers thought I was acting like several kinds of an idiot—"

He launched into a long tirade while I got another cigarette going. He was bragging now, boasting about a deal he had pulled off years ago, and he seemed to like the sound of his own voice so much that I let him listen to it as long as he wanted to. During the war, it seemed, he had bought a ring of property around the perimeter of the city. He bought it cheap, and he was sitting on a whole boatload of it when the postwar housing boom hit at the end of the war. Then he had gone and done the same thing during Korea, with results almost as spectacular.

"I'm getting off the track again. What I mean, John, is that you people are buying up this land for no price at all. Now take my acreage. You offered me five hundred dollars for it, is that right?"

"Yes, and—"

"And do you want to know something? It didn't occur to me for the longest time to stop and figure out what the right market price for that land is. I always knew it was a good sum short of what I had in the property, but I never bothered to pinpoint it. Well, I finally did, and do you know what my land actually ought to be worth?" I didn't answer him.

"Between two thousand and twenty-five hundred dollars," he said triumphantly. "And here you were trying to steal all of that for no more than five hundred."

I drew myself up straight in my chair. "I don't think you can call that stealing," I said stiffly. "That was a bona fide offer, Wally, and whether or not you happened to like the price—"

"Now hold on." He got up from his chair, came out from behind the desk. He gripped my shoulder and I let myself relax. "Just take it easy," he was saying. "No one's calling you a thief."

"That's what it sounded like."

"Well, then, I apologize. Is that better?" I let that go. He told me he certainly didn't want to get on the wrong side of me. After all, we were both Americans, weren't we? I might be working for a Canuck outfit, but, damn it, I was a New Mexico boy, and New Mexico and Olean were a lot closer to each other than either was to Toronto, weren't they? They weren't on any map that I knew about, but he was talking and I let him have all the room he needed. "Here's where it gets funny," he said. "See, I know what this Barnstable outfit's been doing. Damned if I don't admire the whole operation, John. If anybody wanted to pick up land at a good price, you couldn't ask for a better way of doing it."

"And perfectly legal," I reminded him.

"Oh, perfectly legal." He smiled momentarily. "But to get back to what I was getting at. Here I've got the whole thing figured out, what you people are doing and all, and then I run into a snag. Because I'll be damned if I can figure out what you intend to do with the land."

I didn't say anything.

"Purchase and development of western territory," he quoted. "That's the alleged purpose of your incorporation, John."

"It is?"

He chuckled. "Didn't know that yourself, did you? But that's the way you boys worded it in your application for a charter. I'm willing to dig a little for information, see? Purchase and development. That might make a little sense, except as far as I can see you folks aren't in any position to do any development, and developing the quantity of land you've bought would be one hell of an expense. You know what the total capitalization of the Barnstable Corporation is?"

"As a matter of fact, I don't."

"No reason why you should. It happens to be fifty thousand dollars, which might sound like a good sum of money but which, believe me, is a damned small figure in an operation like this one. Why, John, I'd be willing to bet that you people have spent close to that much just on land."

"How did you—"

"Why, as I said, John, I have my ways of getting information. Now there are various possibilities

involved. You—I don't mean you personally, I mean
Barnstable—you might have set up this corporation
just for purchase itself, and then you'll do the actual
development through another corporation so that you
can work out a nice capital gain picture for yourselves.
That's one possibility. Or you might augment capitalization once you've got your land purchased, and then
you'll float a stock issue or have all the stock holders
increase their investment."

I didn't say anything. He walked over to the window
and yawned and stretched and looked at his watch and
said that it looked like that time again, and could I use
a drink? I thought it over and started to say that I
didn't think so.

"Oh, come on," he said. "I can use an eye-opener
myself, so why not join me?"

He had one drawer of a filing cabinet set up as a
makeshift bar. He brought out a bottle of very good
Scotch, poured a couple ounces in each of two glasses,
and added squirts of seltzer from a siphon.

"British style," he said. "No ice. That how they
drink up in Canada?"

"Well, I guess most people take ice."

"That's something," he said.

We worked on our drinks. He set his down and
said, "You know what bothers me? Even figuring that
you'll recapitalize after you've bought as much land as
you want, even figuring that, I can't make out why the
hell you would want to develop that land now. What
the hell can you do with it? You can't build a row of

houses out there and expect anybody to buy them. Dammit, I checked what's planned for that area, and there's no prospect of growth there for years and years. It's still wasteland. It may be worth a couple hundred dollars a square mile and you're buying it at forty dollars a square mile, so you're certainly getting it at the right price, but what the hell are you going to do with it?"

I had some more of my Scotch and made circles on his desk top with the glass. I lit a cigarette and shook out the match.

"Wally," I said, "why are you so interested in finding out?"

"Can't you guess?"

"I know you got interested because we expressed interest in your land. But it's pretty obvious by now that you're not going to sell to us, and that we wouldn't be interested in raising our offer, so why stay excited about it?"

"You mean why poke my nose in?"

"Well, I wouldn't put it that way—"

"You ought to, John, because that's what I've been doing. I've been poking my nose into something that's not my business. No getting around that."

"Whatever you want to call it," I said.

"I suppose I've got a reason."

"Oh?"

He finished his drink. He pursed his lips and narrowed his eyes and did all those little facial tricks that were supposed to show that he was ready to get down to brass tacks, that he was prepared to talk sincerely about something of prime importance.

"John," he said, "I smell money."

We both paused reverently to let that sink in. He picked up his cigar and put it down again and said, "John, somebody's setting up to make a pile of money out of a load of moose pasture. I've always been interested in money. And ever since I got raped by those Canadian sharpies you can bet I've been interested in moose pasture. If there's a way to make a nice chunk of dough out of that land, I'd like to know about it. You can appreciate that, can't you?"

"I guess I can."

"If you've ever been swindled, you know what I mean. It's damn hard for a man to swallow his pride and say the hell with it, he's been taken. A real man wants to get back. Not just to get even, but to come out of the whole thing smelling like a rose. And there's something going on here with Barnstable, and I can't get away from the feeling that there's an opportunity here for Wally Gunderman. You blame me for being interested?"

"I don't know what good it can do you," I said levelly.

"Don't you?"

"Well, frankly, no. I don't."

He thought it over for a moment. "Maybe if you told me a little, John. If you filled in the gaps for me, maybe we'd both know a little more where we stand."

"Anything I know is confidential," I reminded him. "I already told you more than I should have."

"Now, John, you and I both know you never told me a thing."

"Well, what I let slip to Evvie, then. Your secretary." I swallowed. "If Mr. Rance or anybody else in Toronto learned that I had too much to drink and then shot off my mouth—"

"You didn't say a thing I wouldn't have found out anyway, John. And I had already decided to find out what was going on, so I would have done my digging even if you never said a word to the girl." He winked slyly. "Besides, John, I'm not about to tell your Mr. Rance or Mr. Whittlief or anyone else about our conversations. You can trust me, John."

I brightened a little. He took my glass and freshened both our drinks without asking. I sipped mine and he lit his cigar again and sighed heavily. I looked at him.

"John," he said, "I don't mind saying that I'm glad you're the man they sent down here. There are certainly men in the world who might talk more freely than you do, but one thing is sure. When you finally do open up, I'm able to believe what you tell me. If you're not prepared to tell the truth, why, you just don't say anything at all, do you?"

"Uh—"

"The thing is that I feel I can trust you to play straight with me, and that's an important thing." He lowered his eyes. "I hope you feel the same way about me, John."

"Of course I do."

"Because I'm a man who deals honestly with people. If someone plays fair with me, you can bet that I'll play fair with him. And when somebody does me a favor, or helps me out in any way, you can be damned certain that I'll see he's taken care of and properly. When I have dealings with a man, he has no cause to regret it, and you wouldn't either, John."

I think I probably looked slightly lost just then. It wasn't all acting. He was approaching the whole question from about five different angles all at once. He had the ball, and he was damn well ready to run with it, but he wasn't too certain where the goal posts were and he was tearing off in several directions without knowing exactly where he was headed. He wanted to win me over, and he wanted to learn what Barnstable was going to do with its land, and he wanted, somehow, to find a way to cut a piece of the pie for himself.

And I wasn't sure how much to give him at once. He was a tricky guy. This was good—the con we had going for us would only work against a shrewd man. There's an old maxim to the effect that you cannot swindle a completely honest man. I'm not sure this is entirely true—it would be hard to test it empirically, because I don't think I have ever met an entirely honest man.

But there is truth to it, and there is a corollary argument: You cannot pull certain cons against stupid men. In the more elaborate long cons, you need to use the mark's native intelligence and shrewdness against him. It's a sort of mental judo.

At any rate, I had to admire Gunderman, at least in

certain respects. He was doing a good job of roping me. First he made me feel foolish for blabbing to Evvie, then he let me know that I could trust him, that he wouldn't let Rance know what I'd done. Right away this made us co-conspirators and set the groundwork for future conspiracy. He wasn't as smooth as he could be, and he made his own position a little too obvious, but I had to give him credit; for an amateur, he wasn't that bad a con artist.

Now he said, "John, you don't mind a personal question, do you?"

"I guess that depends on how personal it is."

"Well, why beat around the bush? I'll come right out and ask you. How much money do these Barnstable people pay you?"

I hesitated. Then I said, "Well, around two hundred a week."

"A little less than that, isn't it?"

"A little."

"About one-eighty?"

"How did you—"

"Well, I didn't inquire directly, John. It came out in the wash. That's one-eighty Canadian, and with the discount that means you're earning something like a hundred and sixty-five a week. I'll tell you, John, that isn't much for someone doing the work you do. And all the traveling and responsibility."

"The travel expenses are paid for me."

"Oh, I know that, naturally. But you still ought to be worth more than that."

"I manage on my salary."

"Of course you do. But if you could pick up a piece of change for yourself, why, you wouldn't complain, would you?"

I didn't answer that.

"I'm not saying you ought to work against your employers, John."

"I couldn't do anything like that."

"You certainly couldn't, and if I thought you were the kind of man who could, why, I wouldn't want to have any dealings with you. But if you could do me a favor without injuring your employers, that might be something else, don't you think?"

I reached for my drink. He smiled at the gesture, then looked away. Not right now, I thought. Give him a night to think it over some more. Take a little time.

"I'm not sure how much help I could be to you," I said.

"Why not let me worry about that?"

I lowered my eyes and chewed my lip thoughtfully. "I ought to think about this," I said.

"Fair enough. Will you be in town a few days, John?"

I took a breath, then expelled it with the air of someone coming to a minor decision. "Wally," I said, "you must have figured out the main reason I'm here. I don't have to tell you that, do I? That is, I already realized you weren't likely to sell out to Barnstable. That was…well, an excuse for the trip."

"You wanted to see Evvie."

"That's right."

"I understand. And why not let the boss pay for the trip, eh?"

I looked very ashamed of myself.

"Perfectly natural," Gunderman said. He laughed heartily. "But you will stay in town for a few days, won't you?"

"If I can manage it."

"Hell, you can manage it, John." He laughed again. "Why, with all those phone calls I've made to your office, your boss will be sure I'm the hottest prospect on earth. He won't begrudge you a few days in town, and if the deal falls through for him, well, that's just the breaks of the game. You stay here in town, and you take some time to think things through, because I want you to make your own decision, John. And you drop around here, oh, come by tomorrow afternoon, and maybe the two of us can do some more talking and figure out how things are likely to shape up for us. I think we'll both come out of this okay, John."

We both finished our drinks. I rallied a little and told him I was glad we were bringing things out in the open, that the one thing I disliked about the Barnstable job was that I hated to misrepresent myself at all. "The hunting-lodge story," I said. "I'd rather tell people the truth right off the bat, that we're prepared to pay so much for their land and that's all. It's a good deal for a lot of them, Wally. They can write off their tax loss and get the bad taste of a bad deal out of their mouths. I'd rather just tell them that and leave it at that, and I know that's how I would handle things if I were a principal in this deal. But I'm just a hired hand."

He liked the way that sounded. He was very taken with me. I was just the man he wanted me to be. We shook hands and we made arrangements to meet the next afternoon, and I left him there ready to tell Diogenes to put down his lantern and call off his search—Wallace J. Gunderman had just found himself an honest man.

Nine

When Evvie left the office a little after five I was out in front with the motor idling. She came out of the building and over to the car. I stood holding the door for her. She was smiling hugely.

"Aim a kiss at me," she said, behind the smile.

I did. She went on smiling and turned just a little in my arms so that the kiss missed her mouth and caught her cheek. Then in a second she was in the car. I walked around it and got behind the wheel, and away we went.

I said, "You think he was watching?"

"From the front window. That light's red. Why not stop for it and kiss me proper?"

This time there was no audience for the kiss. She made a little choked-up sound and caught at my shoulders with her hands. Our mouths didn't miss this time. She held on, and the wheels went around and came up three bars, jackpot. A horn honked behind us. She slipped away reluctantly and I piloted the rented Impala across the intersection.

"Now that was better," she said.

She was too damned good to be true. The halfway kiss in front of Gunderman's office building would tell him everything she wanted him to know—that I was hot for her, that she was not interested, but that she would play the game through thick and thin to do the right thing for Poppa Wally. I couldn't have named more than eight women in the country who could have played the scene as well, and those eight were girls who were born to the sport.

I told her how good she was. She glowed a little. I asked her where she felt like going for dinner. Nowhere, she said. She had a pair of filets at the apartment and a hibachi to char them on. How did that sound?

"Home cooking," I said. "You'll spoil me."

"You don't mind? He wanted me to wine you and dine you. He thinks that's the most effective treatment. The big show of money and influence. He knows a few variations, but they're all on the same theme. I told him this would be more intimate."

"It just might."

She didn't answer. I turned a corner and found her block, pulled up a few doors from her building. We went up to her apartment and she unlocked the door. She let me make the drinks while she got the charcoal going in the little Japanese stove. I made stiff drinks. We took them back into the living room with us.

"I don't know," she said.

"About what?"

"Everything, I don't think he's going to fall for it."

"Why not?"

"I'm not sure."

"Did he say something?"

She frowned. "No," she said finally. "It wasn't anything he said, nothing like that exactly. Right now he's completely sold. You've got him in your pocket, John."

"Then what's the problem?"

She thought about it, worked on her drink, looked up at me. "Maybe I'm just worried," she said. "Stage fright."

"Could be."

"It just doesn't seem possible that he'll fall for it. He's not a stupid man, you know. He's less of a clod than he seems. He's got a tough streak of sharpness under it all."

"Then this is tailored for him. A stupid man would never be able to pick up on it."

"I know, but—" She raised her glass to her lips, lowered it again. "I'll tell you something, John. I think you're a little too perfect."

"How do you mean?"

"Too honest and too square. Right now he believes every bit of it. Right now you could probably tell him you're the chief holy man of the Ganges and he wouldn't doubt a word. But he's no believer in the incorruptibility of mankind. If you stay lily-white, he'll start to wonder sooner or later."

"Go on."

"Let him see that you wouldn't mind making a buck. Make him draw it out of you a little at a time, but make sure he knows you're glad to look out for number one as long as it's safe."

I thought it over. "You're right," I said.

"It was just an idea—"

"No. You're right. I may have played it a little too angelic. It's an easy role to fall into." I finished my drink. "Still worried?"

"Of course."

"You don't have to be."

"I'll be worried until this is over. God, if this falls in—" She closed her eyes. "Doug Rance is sitting safe across the border. You can hop on a plane and disappear far enough so that no one will ever find you. And he wouldn't even try too hard. But me—if he ever finds out, John, I've had it. The viper in his bosom." She managed a somewhat brave smile. "He would only kill me," she said.

A whole batch of lines didn't do the job. *Don't worry, everything'll be all right, it's in the bag*—you don't throw phrases like those at a woman who's telling you how she stands a fair chance of getting killed. You don't say anything at all.

I kissed her. She held back at first, too much involved in dreams of doom to ride it all the way. Then the fear broke and she came to me, and the wheels went around again and the slot machine paid off again. There was nothing casual about it.

I took her on her living room couch with her blouse half off and her skirt bunched up around her waist. The couch was too short, engineered for more sedate pleasures. The lights were all too bright. None of this mattered much.

Afterward, she got up to throw our steaks on the fire. I lit us a couple of cigarettes and made a fresh pair of drinks. We didn't talk much. It wasn't necessary.

"What do I do when this is over, John?"

"Take the money and run."

"And then?"

I had my arm around her. I drummed my fingers against the curve of her shoulder. "According to Doug," I said, "you've got a program figured. Meet a rich man and marry him."

She was silent.

"Something wrong?"

"I've already got a rich man. And it wouldn't be very different being married to him. I'd just feel like a whore with a license. I don't know what I'll wind up doing. Right now I can't think very much past a day or two after tomorrow."

We were listening to an Anita O'Day record. Some song about a nightingale. The mood was as mellow as that girl's voice. We could have used a fireplace with thick logs burning. And some very old cognac.

I said, "You could always stay with the grift." I made it light.

"Me?" She laughed softly. "I'd shake apart into little pieces."

"Not you."

"The way I've been?"

"You've been beautiful," I told her. "The nervousness doesn't mean a thing. Anyone who knows what he's doing and cares how it turns out gets nervous."

"Even you?"

"Me more than most."

"You don't let it show."

"It's there, though."

She found a cigarette. I lit it for her. "Would you work with me again on something like this? I mean if I weren't a part of it to begin with. If I was just another hand in the game. Would you want me in on it?"

"Any time."

"Then maybe I've got a career after all. We'll be partners."

"You're forgetting something."

"Oh?"

"I'm about to retire," I said. "Remember?"

"I didn't forget." She drew on her cigarette, took it from her lips, stared at its tip. "I wasn't sure whether or not that was the truth. About quitting, buying that roadhouse."

"Does it sound pipe-dreamish?"

"That's not it. I thought it might be part of a line. It sounded sincere enough at the time, but later, well, you're very good at sounding sincere. Will you really do it, John?"

"Yes."

"And you're sure you can make a go of it?"

She didn't have to coax me. I was not exactly playing hard to get. I swung into a reading of The Dream, the unabridged version. She kept her head on my shoulder and said the right words at all of the right places. I was long sold on the dream myself, but now it was coming out rosier than ever.

"Colorado," she said. "What's it like out there?"

"You've never been West?"

"Well, Las Vegas and Reno. But that's not the same, is it? All bright lights and no clocks in the casinos and lots of small men with eyes that never show expression. What's Colorado like?"

"Nothing like Vegas."

"Tell me about it."

So I talked about air that lifted you up onto your toes when you filled up your lungs with it, and mountains that climbed straight up and dropped off sharp and clean, and the way the trees turned overnight in early October. I probably sounded very chamber of commerce. I'm apt to get that way. I've always loved that kind of country. The grift always kept me in the cities, mostly on the Coast, because that was where the action was. But I never really felt I was breathing in the cities, especially in the smog belt. And in Q there were times, a couple of them, when I found myself gasping like a trout in a net. The prison doctors said it was psychosomatic. They were probably right. It still had felt very damned fine to be back in the mountains.

Anita stopped singing somewhere in the middle of the lecture, and some clown came on the radio with a fast five minutes of news. Evvie switched off the radio and came back and put her head on my shoulder where it belonged and listened some more. When I finally ran out of gas she didn't say anything. I was a little embarrassed. It's hard to talk like a poet without feeling like a jackass.

Then she said, "You make it sound pretty."

"It is."

"You even make it sound…possible. Quitting the racket, doing what you said."

"It's more than possible, Evvie."

She said, "I wish—" And let it hang there.

First in Q, and then on the outside, there had been many versions of The Dream. Step by step it focused itself and narrowed itself down. Finding Bannion's had been a final touch. Each version of The Dream had become just a shade more specific than the last.

Each version had had The Girl. Sometimes she was formless, and other times she was remarkably well drawn. Sometimes she was a glorious innocent, and she either accepted my past and forgave it or else she knew not a thing about it. In other versions she was a trifle soiled herself—a grifting girl, or a halfway hooker, or any of a dozen shadow-world types. Part of the past, but with me in the future.

But every version had The Girl.

And I heard myself saying, "It wouldn't be exciting. But excitement wears thin after a while. It's good country, Evvie. You'd love it out there—"

She stood up, walked across the room. I sat where I was and listened to my words bouncing off the walls.

She said, "You're not conning me, are you?"

"I don't think I could."

"Because that was starting to sound alarmingly like a proposal."

"Something like that."

She turned. She looked at me, straight at me, and I drank the depths of her eyes. Then she began to nod, and she said, "Yes. Oh, yes, yes."

I saw Gunderman in the morning. I did not much want to see him. I was not in the mood to play a part. The night with Evvie had flattened out the hunger pains, and a hungry man makes a better fisherman.

But the hook was already set, the line already strung halfway across the lake. Even a well-fed angler can reel in a big one, especially when the fish practically jumps into the boat. My heart was not exactly in it, but it did not exactly have to be. Gunderman made it easy.

I followed Evvie's hunch. When I got around to telling him that Barnstable had bought about as much land as was likely to be available at their price, I stopped for a moment and then let on that I would be out of a job before long. "They'll let you go, John?"

"They won't have anything for me to do." I looked off to the side for a second, then lowered my eyes. "Oh, I'll find something else," I said. "I generally do."

"Have money saved?"

"Not a hell of a lot. On my salary—"

"Be handy if you did, though."

"Well," I said, "I'll manage."

He had Evvie bring us some coffee from around the

corner. He stirred sugar into his and got back on the main theme, the opening for one Wallace J. Gunderman. First, of course, he wanted a chance to buy some stock in Barnstable. I told him he didn't have a chance in a hundred. In the first place, no one would be anxious to sell. In the second, the board would never approve of a stock transfer. Everything was very hushed up, I explained. Even I could figure out that much. They were not looking for publicity. Legal or not, they wanted to keep a lid on things.

"What are they going to do with that land, John? Suppose that they haven't got any development planned. What are they going to do?"

"I've thought about that," I said.

"So have I. What did you come up with?"

"Just a few ideas." I stopped long enough to light a cigarette. "At first I thought they were buying for some corporation. It was so hush-hush I figured they had an important client who didn't want anyone to know what was coming off. But they were buying at random. And there would be one little piece of land in the middle of a few of their tracts, and instead of pushing hard to buy it they would let it go if they didn't get it at their price."

"I'm with you so far, John."

"So they have to be buying for themselves. Especially with so many important people involved. And the secrecy, well, they may be doing something legal but they're still playing around in someone else's mess."

"And so they're wearing gloves."

"Right." I drank some of my coffee and made rings on the desk top with the coffee cup. "I suppose they'll just sit on the land," I said. "Just sit and wait until it catches fire pricewise, or until someone wants it enough to give them a pretty profit."

His eyes narrowed. "Would they sell some of it now?"

"To you?"

"To me."

"I don't think so."

"Why not?"

"I don't think it's what they have in mind. I don't really know too much about that end of the operation, actually. I've spent most of my time here in the States. My only real contact is through Douglas Rance, and he doesn't spend too much time filling me in on the subtleties of company policy." I let a little more bitterness edge forward. I was still Little Boy Loyal, but I wasn't as important as I would have liked to be.

He said, "You could probably find out a few things, if you tried. I'd make it worth your while, John."

I looked at him. Wary, but hungry.

"If it turns out that I can make a deal, I'll cut you in. You wouldn't have to lay out any cash, and you'd be in for a full five percent of any profit I might make."

"Well—"

"How does that sound?"

"It sounds very generous, but—"

"And that five percent could be a healthy sum,

John. I'm not talking nickels and dimes, you know."

"I know."

"Will you go to bat for me, then?"

I pursed my lips and took my time. I said, "But if you don't wind up making a deal—"

He'd thought of that. He wanted me as a sort of partner in the operation, but he knew I would have expenses and he wouldn't want me to take a beating. He passed an envelope across the desk. I hesitated, and I let wariness and greed mingle in my expression, and I took the envelope. After all, Evvie was right. I had to be a little bit on the make or he just would not believe I was real.

"Deal?"

"Deal," I said.

There was, I found out, an even five hundred dollars in the envelope. If he'd had any class he'd have made it a thou.

I'd told him I was taking an afternoon flight back to Toronto. I had told Doug the same thing. I did not go back to Toronto. That morning a girl with a husky voice and deep circles under her eyes had asked me to spend another night in Olean. She did not have to ask me twice.

I went back to her apartment. She had given me a spare key, and I waited inside for her to finish work and come home to me. Around four-thirty I called a Chinese restaurant and ordered up some chow mein. I called around until I found a grocery that delivered, and I had a six-pack of beer sent up along with a carton of her brand of cigarettes. We couldn't eat out, and I didn't want to make her cook a meal again.

The table was set when she opened the door. I opened two cans of beer. We ate in the kitchen. The Chinese food tasted as though it had come out of a can. But the beer was cold, and the company was divine.

We didn't talk too much. She wanted to know how much longer it would take, how long it would be before we scored and blew him off once and for all. It was going to take longer than I wanted to think about—not until we scored, necessarily, but until I had a chance to see her again. After the grift was over, she would have to cool it for a while in Olean before she grabbed a westbound plane. This was all something I didn't want to think about, or talk about.

"I feel better about it today," she said. "Not so nervous."

"It must be love."

"Maybe that's part of it."

"It must be."

I had a second beer. She was still on her first. She went into the living room, switched on the radio. A newscast—someone chattered about some new foreign crisis. She turned the dial and found some music. I left the table and grabbed her and kissed her. She giggled and shook free and scurried over to the front of the room. She paused at the window, and her face went white.

I started toward her. She held out a hand and warned me off.

"His car," she said. "Oh, God."

"So I missed my plane and decided to stay over."

"No, it's no good. The dishes—"

I moved fast enough for both of us. I scooped up my dishes and my beer and my pack of cigarettes and my lighter and ducked into the bedroom closet with them. I stood there holding onto everything while her clothes blanketed me. They all carried the smell of her. I was dizzy with it.

He knocked. She opened the door. They spent five or ten minutes in the living room. I could hear snatches of their conversation, not enough to add the stray phrases together and come up with something intelligible. I waited in the closet like a refugee from a French bedroom farce. The humor of it was lost on me. I wanted to grab the son of a bitch and push his face in.

Then they came closer, from living room to bedroom, and now that I could follow the conversation I no longer wanted to hear it. Wallace J. Gunderman was in the mood for love.

She said something about a headache. He said something about girls who had convenient headaches all the time. She said it wasn't like that at all. He said, and she said, and he said, and they wound up in the hay and I had to stand there and listen to it.

It is not supposed to bother you. It is, after all, part of the game; a con artist can no more be jealous of his girl's mock-lovers than a pimp can resent his lady's clients. You are not supposed to give a damn. It is, after all, business and nothing more. It is push-button sex, it means nothing, it is, in fact, part-and-parcel of The Game.

I wanted to kill him.

When he was through I heard her saying something about a headache, a really bad headache, and maybe it would be better if he left her alone. He didn't seem to mind. He had gotten what he came for, what he paid for. He was a long time getting dressed, but he left, finally, and I heard his heavy feet on the stairs.

I crept out of my perfumed closet. She was sitting on the bed, her back to me. I went into the kitchen and put the dishes in the sink. When I came back she faced me and shook her head from side to side.

"I could throw up," she said.

"Easy."

"I'm awful. I'm a damn whore."

"Stop it."

"I am!"

I slapped her harder than I'd intended. Her head snapped back and she put one hand to her face. "That hurt," she said.

"Sorry. But you did what you had to do."

"I know that."

"All right, then."

"But I can't help the way I feel about it. I'm selling myself."

I took a breath. "Maybe," I said. "But just think

what a sweet price you're charging. Because he's going to get hurt. He's going to bleed money."

She brightened up after a while, but the evening was permanently shot. We struggled through an hour's worth of conversation—or five minutes' worth, stretched to fill an hour. Then I put on my jacket and straightened my tie and left. No woman should have to put out for more than one man in one night.

"It'll be a while," I told her. "Call me if anything happens. Or if you get nervous. Or just because you want to." I kissed her and left.

Ten

Doug said, "We must have crossed a wire or two, Johnny. I was expecting to see you yesterday."

"I wound up staying an extra day." I stirred my coffee. "It looked as though it would play better that way."

"You should have called. I thought maybe a wheel came off." He put a match to a cigarette and winked at me. "You got something going with Evvie?"

"Hardly."

"No? I didn't figure you to pass up something like that."

"Not my type," I said. "And never when I'm working."

He laughed. "Work or play, some kinds of games are always in season. What do you think of her?"

"She's all right."

"Is she holding up her end of it?"

"Sure, I'll give her that." Then, grudgingly, "She's got the talent. She plays the game like somebody who knows the rules."

"Well, that's good."

"She's still getting too damned much of the pie," I told him. "She's getting about double what she ought to get."

"We needed her, Johnny."

I allowed that we probably did, after all, and we let it lie there. We were in a coffeepot around the corner from the Barnstable office. I needed a shave and a shower, but I didn't have to impress anybody just now. I lit a fresh cigarette and finished the coffee and we switched into a rundown on the way the play was heading.

One thing you try hard not to do is lie to your partner. It's not a particularly good policy. You generally have enough lies to keep track of without creating new muddles for yourself.

This was an exception. Evvie didn't want him to know about us, and that would have been reason enough; if he had struck out with the girl, he wouldn't be tickled to hear that I was swinging for the bleachers and connecting. And there was more to it than that.

Evvie and I had suddenly become a team. If he thought of us as a combination, he was going to become very unhappy about the split. It was still the same split, still the same money going into the same pockets, but I knew him well enough to know he wouldn't see it that way. He'd see himself dragging down forty thou while the team of Hayden & Stone walked off with fifty between them.

So I'd let him have the glory. Afterward, when it was all over, it would not matter much any more. Doug would be too busy getting rid of forty thousand dollars over a dice table to worry about his personal prestige. And Evvie and I would be back in Colorado, with Bannion's place in our pockets and the world swinging for us from a yo-yo string. Once it was over, we would have more important things on our minds than Doug Rance.

I signaled our waitress and scouted down two more cups of coffee. Doug wanted to talk and talk and talk; he had to cover every angle of the operation once again to make sure we were rolling free and easy. He didn't have to bother, but he didn't have anything else to do and it's hard to do nothing day after day, putting in your time at the store and waiting for the game to catch up with you.

They always say that the waiting is the hardest time. They always say this on television and in the movies, and they are always wrong; the hardest time, naturally, is when you walk that little tightrope that stretches from just before the score on halfway through the blow-off. That's the hardest time because it's the only time you can get hurt. If things cave in before then, you get the hell out of there. And you stay the hell out of jail.

But the waiting time is when you keep looking for trouble spots, and dreaming of disaster. You can't keep busy because there's nothing for you to do. You have to sit tight and wait, and this is a pain in the neck, and Doug had had enough of it so that he wanted to hash things over more than he had to.

I'd be the same way myself in a few days. We had to let Gunderman hang by his thumbs for a few days, and I could already see where it might begin to get on my nerves.

First I had to wait for Gunderman to call me. He couldn't call me at the office, and I wasn't at my room much, so it took him four days to reach me.

"Not much so far," I told him. "Not enough to call you on, anyway. I did find out two things. I couldn't swear to them, they're just hunches so far, but—"

He broke in. Hurry up, hurry up, tell me everything. He wanted to know it all and know it fast.

"Well, they're definitely buying for the purpose we thought, Wally. They won't develop and they aren't buying as anyone's agent. They're picking up land for capital gain."

"And?"

"And I don't think they want to sit on it very long. I have a feeling that they're looking for a fast turnover."

"How?"

"I don't know."

"If I can get in on this, John—"

I let him swim back and forth with it. He stayed on the phone for another ten minutes asking questions while I told him I didn't know the answers. Couldn't I just come out and ask Rance about it? Not yet, I explained. But was there time? And did I feel I was getting anywhere? Oh, he was all full of questions.

"Better hurry up and get those answers," he said finally, back to his genial old self again. "Better let us both make a pile of money, John. I think my girl Evvie misses you something terrible."

Oh, I could have killed him then. I could have reached through space to strangle him long-distance with the phone cord. I tried to keep all of this out of my voice while I got rid of him, and then I went downstairs and around the corner for a pint of Scotch. I came back to the room and called Evvie. A nightly habit of mine. We talked long enough for AT&T to split their stock again, and we said not a word about Gunderman or Rance or Toronto or Olean. We talked about Colorado.

I left Gunderman hanging for the weekend and a day on either side of it. He left messages for me, and I ignored him. I saw every movie in Toronto. I also saw the insides of most of the bars, and looked at the bottoms of a great many glasses. I slept ten to twelve hours out of every twenty-four. There was not much else to do.

I got him at his office at a quarter after two in the afternoon. I said, "Wally, this is John. I'm afraid you're out of luck."

He wanted to know what I meant.

"I thought there might be a way to get in on the deal, if they were going to dispose of the land. I didn't understand their whole operation. They're planning on selling, Wally, but they intend to move it all at once. The whole thing in one package."

"So?"

"That adds up to quite a deal."

"I'm not interested in nickels and dimes, John."

"You'd go for the whole parcel?"

"At the right price, I'd grab it."

"I'm afraid they've already got somebody, Wally. There's a deal hanging on the fire."

"With who?"

"Someone from the Midwest. A syndicate, as far as I can make out. I don't have every last detail. I've been playing this very close, because I've had to do some detecting from the inside without letting them know what I'm after. It hasn't been that easy."

"Now you know I appreciate your position, John—"

I cut in on him. "But I've got most of the picture. I think—God, I hate to go into all of this over the phone. They plan to get completely out from under. They don't intend to sell the land—"

"What the hell—"

"Wait a minute. They're selling the whole corporation, the whole block of Barnstable stock. There are a lot of tax aspects, and there's the matter of publicity. I wish I could get down to Olean and explain this more openly, but I can't possibly get out of town now."

"Suppose I came up there?"

"That's what I was getting at. Could you come up here?"

"No problem."

"Because there's a chance…I'm trying to think on my feet, Wally, because I wouldn't want you to make the trip for nothing. I hadn't realized you might be in the market for the whole thing. It might run six figures, as far as I can tell."

"I'm good for it. If the value's there, John."

"And there are other aspects, too. But there's a fair chance that the deal is all arranged with the syndicate, and that you wouldn't even have a chance to outbid them. Not that I think they'd be willing to work it with bidding anyway. I'm…listen, this is confusing as hell. Can you come up here tomorrow?"

"Why not tonight?"

"Well, I'd want to check out a few angles. I'll tell you what. Make your flight reservations, and I'll figure on meeting you tonight at the Royal York. If anything comes up, I'll call you back before five o'clock. If you don't hear from me, I'll meet you around nine o'clock. Does that sound good?"

He told me it sounded fine.

The element of confusion was not accidental. It was there for a reason. If things were too smooth, he might begin to wonder who had greased the skids for him. But as long as I was a little uncertain as to which end was up, he didn't have anything to be suspicious about.

Getting him to come to Toronto was basic. When you want to win a mooch, you meet him on his home ground. When you want to put him on the defensive, you take him into your own parlor and keep him off balance. Once he got on that plane, Gunderman was committing himself. As long as he stayed in Olean he could tell himself it was just an armchair exercise, one he could back away from whenever the going got rough. Every commitment of time and space and money drew him in a little deeper. The five hundred bucks he'd slipped me was a partial commitment, but he could write off that kind of money easily enough. The trip would tie him up a little tighter.

I went up to the office. Doug had gone for the day. I picked up a phone and called his apartment. "He's on his way," I told him.

"When's the meet?"

"Tonight. Nine o'clock."

"You'll be good, won't you, Johnny?"

"I'll be beautiful. Want to meet him tomorrow?"

"I don't know." My partner was a little on the nervous side, I decided. "You think that's rushing things?"

"It's hard to say. I can't be sure how he'll go tonight. How much rope to give him."

"Enough to tie him up tight, Johnny." He was silent for a minute. "You play it by ear," he said finally. "If it looks like a good idea, you arrange a meeting tomorrow, a sounding session. You see how he acts, how hungry he seems to you. If he's a little cool about things, then just cool him down some more and send him back to Olean to sit on his money. Invent something about how you wanted him up here to give him the full picture but you can't set up a meeting because the Chicago money is all set to make its pitch. But if he seems ripe, make it that he and I'll get together just so he can let his interest show." He laughed suddenly. "Here I am giving orders," he said. "I don't have to draw you pictures, Johnny. You know the game."

"I know the game."

"If he's ready for it, I suppose tomorrow morning would be the best time. That the way you figure it?"

"Around ten-thirty."

"Sure. I should fill up the store, don't you think? Bring in a boy or two?"

"Sure."

"I'll line them up. You do what you can, Johnny, and it'll be ten-thirty at the office. He was good on the phone, huh?"

"Perfect."

"I think we got him," he said. "Jesus, I hope we do."

I managed to be fifteen minutes late getting to the Royal York. I called his room from the desk. He said he would come right down, and I told him it would be better if we talked in his room. It might not be too good, I said, if anybody happened to notice us together.

He probably thought I was acting a little too much like Herbert Philbrick leading three lives. But he went along with the gag, and I took the elevator to his room.

"Come on in, John," he said, "I called room service, and we ought to have a boy coming up with some Johnny Walker Black any minute. Now don't tell me some sharpies from the corn country are going to cut us out of this pie. I'd hate to hear that."

"Chicago's not exactly the corn country."

"That where they're from? Not gangsters, are they?"

It's funny how a mooch can give you ideas you might never have thought of on your own. I brushed the question aside and made a note to feed the notion to Doug for future reference. Sooner or later we would need a good reason why the pending deal fell in, and that might be the germ of as good a one as any.

I started in on the main business at hand. I began by going over familiar territory. The men who owned Barnstable were not interested in long term gain. They were all important people who had seen a chance for a fast dollar with a quick turnover. They had bought a parcel of land, and now they wanted to get completely out from under, make themselves a neat hundred percent profit, and do all of this without getting any dirt on their hands. They cared enough about their reputations to take less for their holdings than they could get otherwise. That didn't matter to them as much as the kind of deal they arranged, and the kind of people they were dealing with.

"You better slow down, John," he said. "I think our liquor's here."

He got the Scotch and ice and glasses from the bellhop, signed the tab and gave the kid a buck. I let him make the drinks. We got back into the swing of things, and I watched the way he worked on his liquor. He was normally a fairly hard drinker, but he wasn't paying the stuff much attention tonight. That meant he was intent on staying on top of things, and that in turn meant that (a) he was hot for the deal and (b) he was no longer supremely confident. I was glad of it on both counts.

"You talk about how they care what kind of people they're dealing with," he said. "Isn't one man's money as good as the next?"

"They want more than money. They want it kept quiet."

"So? If I got a piece of a sweet deal, I wouldn't be anxious to hire a skywriter to spread the word. Anybody who buys in is going to put a lid on things."

"Not if they want money in a hurry."

"I don't follow you."

I laid it out for him. The buyer Barnstable was looking for had to be someone who was willing to sit for a long time before he took his profit. If he started parceling the land and selling it off right away, things would come out into the open and all of this would work to Barnstable's disadvantage. If the buyer held on for a minimum of two years, there was no problem. But it wasn't easy to find someone who would play it that way. Lots of people might say they would keep the property intact, but then they might turn around and do the opposite as soon as the ink was dry.

"That's one thing that occurred to me," I said. "You might not want to tie your money up that way. At the price they want, an operator could work things so that he turned a profit in ninety days' time. And that's exactly what they don't want."

"Well, hell," he said. "I don't want it either!"

"You don't?"

I let him show me just how obvious it was. Why, he pointed out, long-term holdings in cheap land were right up his alley. He was no fast-dollar operator. If any man on earth believed in holding on for the big killing, he was that man. Why, if he could buy the right kind of land and get it at the right price, he would sit on it until hell turned cold. That was what made it all so perfect. They had the deal that was perfect for him, and he was just the buyer they were looking for.

"I just don't know," I said.

"Don't know what?"

"If you were only someone they knew, Wally. So much of this has to be done on trust. If they can't trust the man they're dealing with—"

"Dammit, don't you think they can trust me?"

"*I* do, but they don't know you. Now—"

"I could sell them. This Rance, is he the top dog there?"

"He runs things."

"Suppose I met him?"

"Well, I don't know."

"Dammit, what don't you know?" He was upset with me. I was obviously trying to put the brakes on things, and he wasn't having any part of it. I was seeing complexities where everything was as simple as rolling off a girl. I admitted that I might be able to arrange a meeting. It would have to be quick, and I couldn't promise anything. I knew that the deal with the

Chicago interests hadn't been finalized yet, but I couldn't guarantee that it wasn't in the bag for them.

"I don't know how well it could work, Wally. The one thing they don't want is someone who's apt to walk in there with a pocketful of lawyers and accountants. They—"

More assurances. His accountant was a glorified bookkeeper and that was all, he told me. His accountant kept the taxes down and the books in order, but he wasn't one of these modern morons who didn't put a nickel in a pay toilet without checking it out first with his accountant. And he didn't need legal advice before he took a leak, either.

I more or less knew this side of him already, through Evvie. But it was good to hear him put it into words of his own.

"What kind of money's going to be involved in this, John?"

I told him I wasn't sure, but it looked as though it would run between a hundred and a hundred fifty thou. I made it sound as though I didn't believe that much money existed. That gave him the chance to play the sum down. Nothing was too expensive for the big noise from Olean. The Scrubland King.

"What kind of terms, John?"

"All cash."

"They won't take any paper at all?"

"Not a chance. It has to be cash. And part of it under the table."

"Is that right?"

"I think so."

He thought it over. "That's not so bad," he said. "Raises the capital gains tax on my end, but that's a long time in the future and there's a thousand ways to dodge that part of it. Thinking up the dodges is the part I leave to the accountants, John. They're a whole lot cuter at that side of the game. But they don't have the imagination for the big decisions. Take away their slide rules and they can't tie their shoes in the morning."

"You wouldn't mind a cash deal?"

"Why should I mind?"

"It means tying up money."

"When the profit is there," he said, "a man's a fool to worry how he ties up his money. Instead of drawing interest he takes his time and makes a profit ten times the size of interest."

I was with him until somewhere around midnight. During the tail end of the evening we did a lot less talking and a lot more drinking. He loosened up some and worked harder on the Black Label. He had the right attitude, and as far as I could tell he had taken all the bait without finding a trace of hook so far. He was doing what we wanted. He was pushing hard to sell himself to Rance.

I had already managed to slide a few rough ones past him. I'd dropped the idea in his mind that he might do better playing his own hand instead of bringing his accountants and lawyers too far into the thick of things. This was his style anyway, but it didn't hurt to reinforce it. And I'd set him up for the big hassle of an all-cash deal.

We had considered other possibilities. We had thought about increasing the size of the mythical corporation, inflating our sales price to around a million, taking a hundred thou in cash and paper for the balance. Doug had liked it that way. He thought Gunderman would salivate at the notion of all that profit to be handled with an outlay of a hundred thousand.

I liked it the other way. If the deal was too big, he'd want to look at it a lot harder. To Gunderman, a hundred thousand dollars was a lot less than a million, even if the cash outlay was exactly the same. We wanted to keep him in love with the deal and entranced with the possibilities, but we didn't want him so shaky at the idea of all that money that he would take too long a look at the weak points of our house of cards.

On top of everything, there was something sweet about the notion of the all-cash deal. It fit into the hush-hush aspects of the game. It added, oh, maybe a touch of reality. And by balancing it off against the bit about paying part of the price sub rosa, it all fell right into place. Oh, I liked it fine.

By the time I left his hotel room I knew he'd have to meet Rance in the morning. It made no sense to leave him hanging as much as an extra day. He was set up perfectly now, the timing was ideal, and we couldn't pick a better psychological moment to get this part out of the way. It's tricky when you shift the mooch from the roper to the inside man. You have to handle it just right. Tomorrow was fine.

"I'm their man," he was still telling me as I left. "They couldn't find a more logical person to deal with if they looked forever. I've got a batch of arguments to use on Rance. One man's better to deal with than a whole mob, dammit. When you want to keep things on the quiet side you don't negotiate with a whole army. I can tell him a hell of a lot. I can sell myself, John."

You can sell yourself down the river, I thought. But I just gave him some good sound brotherly advice. Don't push too hard, I told him, and don't rush things. He nodded soberly. He'd be careful, he assured me. He'd do his best.

Eleven

I called Doug that night just to go through the motions with him. I went back to my hotel, figuring I had enough Johnny Black in me to sleep. It turned out I figured wrong. In the morning I would be handing the ball to Doug Rance and it would be my turn to sweat it out on the bench. I got nervous in advance. Sometimes this is good; you get your worrying out of the way and keep cool later on. But I wasn't in the mood for it.

I smoked a few cigarettes and kept reaching for the phone and changing my mind. She'd be sleeping by now. I had no real reason to wake her, nothing to tell her that wouldn't keep. Around two-thirty I gave up, showered, shaved, got dressed and went out. The wind had a sharp cold edge to it. I found an all-night place, had coffee and a ham sandwich. The coffee wasn't bad. I chain smoked and smelled my sweat, the special perspiration of very late hours. A human body too long without sleep, held awake by nerves and little more, is somehow unclean no matter how recent its shower or how close its shave. I had cold feet, and literally so; it was damp down there, with not enough blood circulating.

The greasy spoons draw a greasy crowd at that hour. There were a few night workers, but only a few; Toronto, big and bustling, is still a daylight city. There were drunks either sobering up or waiting for the bars to re-open—it was anybody's guess. There were men and women who had no particular place to go and no pressing reason to go to sleep. There were two or three women who might have been prostitutes and three teenagers who were either faggots or junkies. Sometimes you need a scorecard. Everything looks alike these days.

I lit the last cigarette in the pack and thought about the air in Colorado.

When I was a kid I told stories. People called it lying. It really wasn't; I had a fairly wicked imagination and a tendency to embellish things. I got punished occasionally, but I was not always caught. I became a fairly good liar.

I read some psychology years later in Q. I had remembered something from a college psych course that I wanted to check out, and in the prison library I learned that I had not been what they call a pathological liar. I was always aware that my stories were not true. I was simply good at the game.

So skip a few years. I got fair grades in school—they wrote things like *Could do better with effort* on the margins of the cards. My guidance counselor tried to talk me out of applying to Yale. I had visions—Yale, Yale Law, an apprenticeship with some genius like

Geisler or Leibowitz, then back to New Mexico to be the hottest criminal lawyer on the rapidly expanding frontier. Sometimes in the dreams I wound up staying in the big city. Sometimes I went into politics. I always came out Very Important.

Yale turned me down. I wound up at the state university at Santa Fe and coasted for most of three years. I don't remember many of the courses that I took. I was pre-law, but that generally leaves you a lot of room.

Oh, hell. I couldn't stay off probation. During my junior year there was a girl—there is always a girl—and I buckled down and tried harder. We had it figured. I was going to go to Yale Law, she was going to marry me and work to put me through law school, and then segue into the dream for a big finish, hearts and flowers, over and out.

Everything hit the fan at once. Yale Law said no by return mail, the girl missed her period and got scared, and although it turned out to be a false alarm it managed to kill things for us. I went on a too-long drunk and came out of it in time for a mid-term. I wasn't prepared for it, and they caught me with the book open on my lap.

Maybe I could have talked myself out of it. I didn't try, didn't even wait for the news that the Dean wanted to see me. I could have gone home. You always can, they say, but you don't realize this until later. I did not want to go back to Springer. I did not want to make up a fresh story en route and look at their faces and wonder whether or not they believed it. I packed one suitcase and went into town. I started off flat broke, and the few things I hocked—my typewriter, my radio—did not fatten my wallet.

In the Greyhound station men's room I put on my good suit and a clean shirt and a tie. I checked my suitcase and let a yassuh-boss kid shine my shoes. Then I went shopping in the best department store in Santa Fe.

I spent half an hour in the second-floor men's department. I looked at a few suits and some sport jackets. I tried things on but didn't buy much, just a couple of shirts and a five-dollar tie. I paid cash and looked at my watch while the clerk was wrapping the packages. The California bus was due to take off in fifteen minutes.

"Better hurry it," I said. "I've got a bus to make."

He gave me my package and my change. I walked quickly to the escalator, and I took one step, and then I fell down the full flight and landed in a heap on the floor.

It caused quite a stir. I stayed put for the first few seconds and let them make a fuss over me. One woman had screamed tentatively while I was falling, and then a bevy of nervous clerks made properly nervous sounds. I gave them a minute, then shook my head groggily, gulped air, said something unintelligible, started to get up, stopped, got up, slipped, righted myself, and stood there finally looking as out of it as I possibly could.

They hustled me into the manager's office as fast as they could. If anything had been wrong with me this would have been a very bad move, but they were not anxious to have me lying sprawled out at the foot of the escalator; it was rotten public relations. They sat me down and checked me inexpertly for broken bones and asked me how I felt.

"Gee," I said, "I don't know. My back's twisted all to hell and gone."

"It probably shook you up. You should watch your step, son."

You watch your stepson, I thought. I'll watch my fairy godmother. But what I said was, "I could swear that stair moved when I stepped on it."

"Of course it did. It's an escalator."

"No, the tread slipped sideways. I put one foot square on it and it slipped sideways and I...whew, that was some feeling."

The silence was almost embarrassing. I looked at my watch. It had broken in the fall, and I mentioned this. I asked what time it was. They told me.

"Oh, terrific," I said. "I just missed a bus."

"Where are you going?"

"San Francisco. I live there."

"You go to school at State?"

"That's right."

The room cleared a little. Two of them stayed around, and they played the game as though they knew it very well. Their watch department would repair my ticker free of charge, they explained. And they would put me in a cab to the airport so that I could fly to San Francisco.

That was very decent of them, I said.

"Just sign right here, Mr. Hayden—"

I got the pen almost to the paper, then stopped. "Wait a second," I said. "Suppose I really racked myself up?"

"Well—"

"Listen, my roommate's old man is a lawyer. He's got this big negligence practice in Albuquerque. The stories Ray told me, say, I'm not signing *anything*."

They would fix my watch and put me in a cab? Sure they would. I put the pen down and they opened up a little. Nobody wanted to talk about lawyers, I was assured. Nobody wanted to spend weeks or even months in a courtroom. I was all right, and if anything turned up I had his personal guarantee that my medical expenses would be taken care of, but it was very important to him personally that they get the paperwork out of the way. All they needed was my signature.

They sweetened the pot. Just as a token of their concern for my welfare, they would throw in a suit. I could pick any suit in the store, with their compliments.

"Well, I already *looked* at every suit in the store," I told them, properly baffled. "I couldn't find anything I even *wanted*, for God's sake. I mean, my Dad buys me all the suits I want."

I let them make the deal. We closed for a new watch, air passage to S.F., and a flat hundred bucks in cash. I wrote my name on the line and that was that.

It was all very easy. Later on I couldn't believe how easy it had been, how gently I had slipped into the role, how stupid they were. The idiots thought they were being so goddamn smooth about everything. Greasing the skids for me, making me sign myself out of a six-figure nuisance suit for a few bucks and a watch and an airplane ticket. They danced for me like puppets, and they were so busy being cute they never even felt the strings.

The only hard part was at the beginning. Pitching myself down that escalator—that took a little doing. But from there on it was gravy. The first step was a lulu, but the rest of the road was a cinch.

And that, I suppose, was the beginning. I pulled the same dodge a week later in a San Francisco department store and found out I'd had a large dose of beginner's luck. I took a fairly bad fall to start things off, and then I ran up against a floor manager who pegged me for a grifter from the go. As it turned out, I had to spend a week in the hospital. I actually went ahead and got a Market Street lawyer to take the case. This surprised the hell out of the floor manager. I turned out to be one hundred percent clean, a hard-working college dropout with no criminal record and no shady past history whatsoever. They got religion and settled out of court. After I paid the lawyer and the hospital I had almost eighteen hundred dollars to cushion me.

I also had one grift I could never pull again for the

rest of my life. Nor was I inclined to. That was one
nasty fall on that escalator.

There were other angles.

With eighteen hundred dollars I was in no particular hurry to find a job. Knock around for a while with
time on your hands and the right gleam in your eye
and you meet people. Meet the right people and you
learn the business. If the life doesn't fit, it's not long
before you drop it or it drops you and you look for a
calmer way to make a living. If it fits you, then
you're home.

I used to think about this in Q. I had worlds of
time for thought. I tried to work it back to the beginning, like tracing a river to its source. When I was a
kid in geography class I thought rivers had sources
that were very dramatic affairs—clear streams of
water leaping out of rocks and such. But follow a
river back and it spreads into smaller and smaller
streams. Trace them one by one and they disappear
into acres of dust. The thinking sessions in prison
dried up the same way.

If I hadn't busted out of State I'd have screwed
things up for myself somewhere else along the line. If
I had struck out hard on that first roll down the escalator I'd have found another better angle later on. I
was too good at it, and too given to dreams and lies,
and far too inept at going through life reading the
script.

The crazy things you think of late at night. I never

did get to sleep. I drank coffee until it backed up on me and I got a little shaky. I took a long walk in the false dawn and watched the city yawn and wake up. I went back to the hotel, showered again, changed clothes again, and had a respectable breakfast. Before too long it was time to pick up my pigeon and show him the coop.

Twelve

The store was swinging in full-dressed splendor by the time I got Gunderman there. The night before, Doug had called our Manpower secretary and told her to take the day off. Then he made other calls and hired us a batch of day-workers.

With Gunderman actually coming to the office, we had to be able to stand a genuine white-glove inspection. We had to present the illusion of real activity. To do this, we needed people. And, because we were dealing strictly in illusion, we needed people who could play their assigned roles and keep their mouths shut. People who were with it.

We had two men, local grifters who were presently unemployed and who were not averse to picking up half a yard apiece for doing nothing special. One of them wore glasses and sat behind a desk jockeying a rented adding machine. The other leafed through a stack of newspapers and assorted garbage and dictated meaningless memos from time to time into a rented dictaphone.

Our Manpower girl had been temporarily replaced by a pleasant old girl with salt-and-pepper hair and a touch of Scottish burr to her voice. She was an old girlfriend of Winger Tim. She had since married on the square. Her husband was a few years dead. She lived on insurance money, acted in some Toronto amateur theater group, and did per diem work with grifting mobs when she was needed. We got her at bargain rates, just twenty dollars for the day. But she didn't really need the money. She wanted the excitement.

Everything was staged just about right. When I ushered Gunderman into the outer office, one of our men was working the adding machine while the gal—Helen Wyatt—was talking on the telephone to a dead line. She was explaining that Mr. Rance was not in. She hung up, and I told her that Mr. Gunderman was here to see Mr. Rance. She buzzed Doug to tell him this, and while we waited our other hired hand came into the office, said hello to me, hung his coat on a peg and went to work. This was one of my touches. It is better if the scene changes within the store *while* the mark is present. This keeps him from wondering whether things have been set up for his benefit, all waiting for him to come and see.

I turned Wally over to Doug. My partner followed the script, wasting no time on me, hitting Gunderman with a ray of charm while giving the impression that he really had better things to do than spend time with Olean's answer to William Zeckendorf. They wended their pleasant way into the inner office and I walked over to the front desk and chucked Helen under the chin. "One of these days," I assured her, "you and I are going to have a wild affair."

"Not I. My bones are too brittle."

"A young chicken like you?"

"Don't tease a poor widow lady, John." She sighed theatrically. "I wish I knew what this was all about," she said. "Nobody ever lets me read the whole script. Just my own lines."

I looked her elaborately up and down and assured her that there was nothing wrong with her lines. She told me to go away, and I did. I went to a drugstore around the corner and called the office.

She said, "Barnstable, good morning."

I said, "I had one grunch but the eggplant over there," and she hung up.

I was not calling just to keep Helen happy in her widowhood. This was more of the illusion. Phones ringing show that an office is in contact with the outside world. All of this helps, not on a conscious level but right back at the base of the mark's mind.

The more elaborately you do this, the better off you are. Cutting corners is always dangerous. When a store is set up perfectly, it gives you so great an edge that you can clean your mark and blow him off and leave him so sold that he simply refuses to believe he's been conned, no matter what. I knew a stock mob that set up a bucket shop that came on stronger than any Wall Street office ever did. They had four marks on the string at once, and they scored with three and let the fourth off because it looked as though he might tip. One of the mooches figured things out a few days later, and the police wound up picking up the other two losers and telling them they bad been had.

They had been so well sold that they would not believe it. And when the bulls took one of them by the hand and led him back to the office of that very friendly stockbroker, he wouldn't believe it when the suite of offices turned out to be very empty. He was sure he was on the wrong street. He made the cop check out some other addresses, because he was utterly sold on the legitimacy of that bucket shop.

I kept calling our offices. Not constantly, because we weren't supposed to be all that active. Just often enough so that Gunderman would hear a phone ring every once in a while. He might not take conscious note of it, but it would make an impression.

Once Helen put me through to Doug. I told him the weather was nice and the Yankees were in last place and ontogeny recapitulates phylogeny. He said things like *Mmmmm* and *I don't think so* and *You'd better check it more carefully*. Somewhere in the middle of one of my sentences he told me to call him back, he was busy, and I should go into it in detail. Then he hung up on me and I went and had another cup of coffee.

Then I called again, later on, and Helen told me that our boy was gone. "I'll put Doug on," she said.

"That's a sweet friend you've got," he told me. "Robbing that clod makes me feel like Robin Hood."

"You didn't take a shine to him?"

"I hated him. I figured the frail was exaggerating, but he's even worse than she said."

"How did it go?"

"The right way. Come on up and I'll tell you about it."

"Do you have to?"

"Huh?"

I told him that I hadn't had any sleep. He laughed. "Stage fright? An old hand like you?"

"Partly stage fright, I suppose. Mostly some things I wanted to think about. By the time I felt like sleeping I couldn't, because I had to be able to meet him on time. I've been walking around on adrenalin for a couple of hours and I'm just about out of the stuff. I think I'll sack out and catch you later."

"Good enough. Oh, Johnny—"

"What?"

"Don't go back to your hotel. He told me he has to catch a plane this afternoon. I doubt that he made reservations. You don't want to be asleep at your hotel when he calls. And your desk clerk might screw things up and tell him. Go to a decent hotel and get a good flop."

"Where?"

"Not the Royal York if he's there. Just a minute. Oh, hell—go to my place. You remember how to get there?"

I'd been to his apartment a few times. I told him I remembered where it was.

"The door's open," he said.

"You don't lock it?"

He laughed. "I never lock my door," he said. "I trust people, Johnny. I've found most people are basically honest."

Thirteen

I spent the afternoon and most of the night at Doug's apartment. Our respective roles gave him one substantial advantage. As bossman, he was supposed to live it up in a fairly plush apartment. Lackey that I was, I had to make do with a third-rate hotel.

I was back at my third-rate hotel the next day when Gunderman called me. The operator made sure that I was really me, and then I heard Evvie's voice in the distance telling him that she had John Hayden on the phone, and at last his voice boomed in my ear.

"Where the hell were you yesterday? I stuck around waiting for you to call and calling you and not reaching you, John. I wanted to get together with you before I flew back, and then I tried you last night and couldn't get hold of you. Got a girlfriend to keep you busy?"

"I was tied up during the morning," I told him. "And then Mr. Rance said you'd gone straight back to Olean, so I didn't try you at your hotel."

"Well, I didn't want him thinking how close we're working on this, John. I'll tell you one thing, though. I like this Doug Rance of yours."

"He's quite a man."

"I'll go along with that. I'll bet his background's good. His family. His father had money, didn't he?"

"I believe so."

"It shows. I understand the English say it takes three generations to come up with a gentleman. I don't know if they're not a little off on their timetable, but they've got the idea. You can always tell whether or not you're dealing with someone who's…well, call it quality. I'm as democratic as the next person, John, but I'd be a damned fool if I didn't know there's a difference between a man like Rance and a man whose father cleaned out toilets for a living."

Doug Rance's father didn't clean out toilets for a living.

He was an auto mechanic, fairly competent when he was sober, which was not his natural condition. He was generally out of work, and he bought himself a case of cirrhosis of the liver and died of it. I did not pass this data on to Gunderman.

"I think he liked me, John. Talk to him?"

"Not at length."

"And?"

I hesitated. "I think you've got a very good chance," I said finally.

"Just a chance?"

"For one thing, he'll have to talk to some of the other principals. He can't make decisions entirely on his own."

"If he goes for the deal, the rest of them will follow suit, won't they?"

"I suppose so. But there's that Chicago group. I told you, Wally, I didn't get to talk much with him. I know he liked you and that he was impressed with your approach."

"I just put my cards on the table."

"Well, I guess he liked that. The way I see it, you're right on top of the waiting list. You—"

"Waiting list!"

"That's right. What did you expect? The Chicago people have the inside track. If they hang onto it, they're going to swing the deal. If they drop out, you're home free."

"I don't know if I like that, John."

"Look—"

"You look, damn it. I sat there in Rance's office and we cleared a lot of air. I'll tell you, he didn't know me from Adam, but by the time I left we had accomplished something. We knew each other and we liked each other, and what's more I made him see just how sensible it was for him to deal with me. Now I've got my proposition hanging there and I'm supposed to wait and find out what happens next." He paused, and when he spoke again his voice was pitched slower, his words spaced further apart. "Like proposing to a woman and having her not say yes and not say no, just keeping you waiting until she makes up her mind. A man can tire of that sort of thing."

I said something sympathetic.

"These Chicago people. I hate this sitting and waiting for them to hit or strike out."

"I'm trying to sink their ship. What the hell do you expect?"

"You're trying to—"

I let some impatience show in my voice. "Oh, hell," I snapped. "What do you think I was doing until four in the morning? It's going to take some doing, making them look bad to Rance and the others. I've been trying everything I can think of to throw them off the track. Don't you think I want my cut?" I suspect he'd forgotten my cut. "And don't you think I want to earn it?"

"Well, I'm a son of a bitch," he said. "I never even thought about that end of it."

"I can't think of anything else."

"My apologies, John. You know I appreciate what you've done, not to mention what you're doing. Have you got something good working?"

"I don't want to talk about it now," I said. At least that saved improvising a new bit of material. "Listen, I've got to cut this short. I'll be in touch with you, but don't expect a call every hour on the hour. I'll let you know if anything breaks either way. And don't call me. If there's anything to know, you'll know it."

Doug thought everything was coming up roses. I wasn't that positive now. The phone call bothered me. He'd gotten fairly belligerent at one point, and this served to point up the thin line we had to walk. We had to keep the carrot just the right distance from the donkey's nose. Too close and he might take a sniff

before biting into it. Too far away and he'd get his
hackles up and never bite at all.

So Doug was all for coasting along, then rushing
into it and pulling it off fast and hard. This could not
be. He had to be teased and coaxed, encouraged and
yet held back.

Evvie didn't want me to call her any more. It was
too risky, she said. She would call me when she got the
chance, from some neutral phone so that there would
be no record of the call. This didn't make a world of
sense but I could figure it out. She was starting to
tighten up. We were coming around the far turn and
the pace was beginning to get to her. No surprise
there. She played the game like one born to it, but
talent was never a complete substitute for experience.
This was her first time. Everybody's first time is a
frightening occasion, especially when you're doing
little but wait for the finish. I can still remember the
first long con game I ever worked, my role as minor as
could be, and the sweat I worked up over it all. And by
then I'd already acquired a fair background in the
game. For Evvie, entirely new to it and close to the
center of things, seeing Gunderman day after day, it
had to be hell.

"Maybe you did too good a job," she said the next
night.

"How?"

"He just won't let go of this. He talks about it constantly, John. I don't even understand it. It's not as if
this was going to make him suddenly rich. He's rich

already. What kind of profit does he think he can turn on this?"

"A handy one. That's not the point."

"It's not?"

"He got taken once, don't forget. On a moose pasture dodge. This means getting even and then some. You know the man's pride."

"Of course."

"That's why he won't let go, kitten."

"It just worries me," she said. "I think what would happen if he ever found out. I get shaky thinking about it. And here I thought I was so level-headed and calm and cool."

"You're doing fine."

"Am I? Maybe. I'll tell you something, I don't think I could go through this again. It's not that bad when you know it's one time and one time only. That makes it easier. I couldn't do it again, though. Not ever. You used to do this all the time, didn't you? I don't see how you kept from flying apart."

"You get used to it."

"Are you used to it now?"

I didn't answer immediately. Then I said, "It comes easy. When you know how to do something fairly well and when you've done it for a very long time, it comes easy enough. But no, I don't think I could go back to the life all the way. This is the last one, a final shot at the moon and for a very good reason. I wouldn't want to go through it again."

"I'm—"

"What?"

"I guess I'm frightened, John." A pause. "I wish you could come here. I wish—"

"It won't be long."

"No," she said. "Not long."

We killed him with phone calls. He was under orders, he was not supposed to call me and he didn't dare call Doug. We goaded him like picadors placing darts in a bull.

"John here, Wally. I can only talk for a minute. I think Rance will call you in a day or two at the outside. I think we've got Chicago hanging on the ropes—"

"They're out?"

"About three-fourths out and going fast. I don't even want to talk about the way I've played it, but I don't think Rance will be in a hurry to deal with them. He may not call you, but I think he will. He'll be anxious to talk price."

"You mean he'll deal, finally?"

"Now, I don't think he'll be that firm about it, Wally. He may keep it very iffy. What he'll want to do, if he calls, is settle on a price so that he'll have that much out of the way when the deal is in the final stages. Whatever price the two of you reach, it'll be firm as far as he's concerned when the time comes."

"Do I have room to bargain?"

"I know what he wants."

"How much?"

"He wants a hundred and a half, a hundred fifty

thousand. He wants half of that in cash under the table
and the other half showing on paper. Now, I have a
pretty good idea what kind of a figure you can arrive at
with him. Oh, God. I'll call you back."

"Wait—"

Click.

"Wally—"

"What the hell happened?"

"Company I hadn't figured on. Where was I?"

He told me where I was.

"That's right. I know it's a bargain at his price, Wally,
but I don't think you should have to pay that much.
You ought to be able to get in for less than that."

"I don't want to blow everything for nickels and
dimes, John."

A born mooch. "Don't worry about that part of it.
The thing is, they've got the tax consideration, and
that's important to them. That's why part of the money
has to be under the table, and that's where you have a
big bargaining point."

"I think I see what you mean."

"Sure. You offer less money overall but a higher
proportion in cold cash. That makes it less like hag-
gling, too. They can accept a lower offer without losing
face."

"I follow you."

"Start by saying yes to the full price, Wally. But say
you'll pay that figure on paper, period. Don't worry
about Rance saying yes to it. He won't. He can't."

"And then?"

"Then you come back with a counter-offer. Tell him you'll go more in cash if he wants, but you want a concession on the price. Offer him fifty each way."

"And he'll take that?"

"No, but that should open it up. I think he'll settle for seventy cash and fifty on paper. That's a hundred twenty thousand, and that saves you thirty thousand dollars."

You just have to let them think they're getting a bargain. You have to put them in the driver's seat, and then let them drive over the cliff. When Doug talked to him, he gave Gunderman just a little extra rope. They wound up ten thousand dollars under the figure I'd mentioned. A hundred ten instead of a hundred twenty. I'd supplied good information and Gunderman had showed himself to be a good and proper wheeler-dealer. He'd never dig his way out now. It was piled hip deep all around him, and the fool thought it smelled just fine.

"Wally, I think you should start raising cash."

"Well, what the hell is this, anyway? Just Wednesday—"

"You don't know how these things move. Or what I've been going through. This isn't a promise, but it would be good if you had the cash on you when the time came. Can you get up the dough without being obvious about it? A little here and a little there?"

"Nothing easier."

"You're sure?"

"No problem, John."

No problem at all. Doug called later and told him to raise the money, that he felt the deal was ninety percent firm, that he'd spoken with everyone on the board and every silent partner and all that was needed was the board's formal approval. No problem, none at all. But Barnstable had better make its mind up, he wanted Doug to know. He wasn't handing out an ultimatum, not by any means, but he had another very attractive opportunity open to him and he didn't have the cash to swing them both at once. He'd prefer the Barnstable deal any time, but if they wouldn't close with him soon he might not want to take the chance of losing out entirely.

Not a bad old horse trader, Wallace J. Gunderman. A standard pitch, one you see coming all the way but one you don't want to ignore entirely because it just might be true. A handy way to put on pressure for a closing without seeming to press too hard.

He was good in his element. But we had never been in his element, had never played ball in his league. This was no straight deal. It was a con, and we sat and laughed at shrewd old Wally.

No problem, no problem at all. And on an early-to-bed evening my phone jangled brittly on the nightstand. I cursed Gunderman for waking me and hustled the phone to my ear.

And a kitten's voice said, "Oh, John. Oh, God—"

"What's wrong?"

"Could you get on a plane right away? Could you come here? Maybe I'm crazy, I don't know. Maybe I am. It's risky, isn't it? We shouldn't see each other now—"

"Evvie, calm down."

Silence. Then, "I'm all right."

"What's the matter?"

"I just better see you," she said. "I think he knows. I'm scared to death he knows."

Fourteen

Somehow I beat the sun there. I spilled out of a yawning cabby's hack and dashed up the walk to her door. There was a light on upstairs. I took the stairs two at a time. She met me at the top and collapsed in my arms. She tried to talk and couldn't make it. I got her inside, shut the door. She still couldn't talk. Her eyes were circled in red, her face drawn. She looked like hell. Broken by a life of unquiet desperation. Shredded; wrung out.

I'd done the wrong thing, of course. There are two possible courses of action when things come unglued. If the end is still at all uncertain, you cool it and wait things out from a safe distance. If there is no doubt that the fit and the shan have connected, you fold up your tent and run for cover.

What you do not do, ever, is lead the Light Brigade straight into hell's mouth.

Fine. But my woman had called for help, and the rules were suddenly obsolete. We had been too long apart. She was afraid, and alone. If she was in trouble I had to be with her to get her out. If she was only having nightmares, it was my job to hold her hand.

When she calmed down she said, "I shouldn't have

called you. I guess I'm not as good as I thought I was."

"Easy."

"I think I'm all right now. I wanted to call you back and tell you not to come. It doesn't make any sense. I missed you, and I kept getting more nervous all the time and there was nobody handy to lean on. I'm sorry, darling."

I told her that it was all right. She took the last cigarette from her pack. I gave her a light. She sat close beside me on the couch and smoked.

I said, "You said you thought he knows."

"It was probably my nerves."

"What happened?"

"Partly his attitude. He seems very different. He's a gruff, impulsive man, John, but he's always been even-tempered with me. He blows off steam now and then. Everybody does. But lately he snaps all the time. And the way he looks at me. I catch him looking at me when he doesn't know I can see him. As though he's trying to figure something out, as though he suspects something."

"You're piling up molehills."

"Enough of them could make a mountain, couldn't they?" She knocked ashes from her cigarette, put it to her lips, drew on it. "He needles me about you."

"How?"

"He refers to you as my boyfriend. In a sarcastic way, but with an undertone that gives me the feeling— I don't know, I guess this must be way off-base—"

"Go on."

"As though it's a joke but he means it anyway. Do you know what I mean?"

"He's kidding on the square."

She nodded gratefully. "As though he has things figured out with almost all of the pieces in place. And he's going along with it, waiting to see what happens, and ready to tear us apart at the end. I'm so *scared* of him. He would kill me. Just like that."

Her hands were shaking. I took her cigarette and put it out for her. I told her she was adding it up and coming out all wrong.

"Well, what does it mean?"

"It first of all doesn't mean what you think. It's too far out of character. Even if he decided to stick around for the ending once he tipped to the con, he wouldn't play it this way. He'd be poking around everywhere trying to fit all the pieces together. He'd be on the phone with me trying to trap me up. He thinks he's very good at that. He would push it."

"I didn't think of that."

"Besides, I know how sold he is. I've been playing him slow for a reason, baby. Slower than Doug would like, all to make sure that nothing will shake him loose. Don't you know why he's acting the way he is?"

"Why?"

"Because he has to have it all. Everything. He can't stand to give a thing away. Not money and not people either. He used you as bait to get me into this thing. Now it bothers him. He can't get rid of the feeling that maybe you gave me a little too much. You belong to him, see? It's all right for him to use you as a teaser, but he doesn't like the idea that maybe you got carried away with yourself and crawled into the rack with me."

She was nodding slowly. "He needed you to get me into it on his side, but he's conveniently forgotten that by now. I think he's forgotten that I'm supposed to be cut in for five percent of his action. He never put it on paper, naturally, and I'm damn sure he'd edge out of it if I ever asked for the dough. He's not exactly the last of the big spenders. He sweetened things a while back with a half a thou for my expenses. Anyone with class would have doubled that figure, minimum. But he's cheap. He picks up dinner checks and he doesn't turn off the lights to save electricity, but he's still a stingy son of a bitch."

"Well, that's the truth."

I went on like that, giving her every reason on earth why there was nothing to be afraid of. They weren't all of them logical, but the more I could throw at her the cooler she would be for the rest of the distance. I must have sounded a lot more sure of myself than I actually was. A score is never a sure thing until the cash is in hand and the mooch a thousand miles away. There's never been one yet that didn't have a chance of going to hell on crutches.

But I talked, and she listened, and it seemed to sink in. She asked me if Doug knew I'd come down. I said I hadn't had a chance to tell him, and wouldn't have bothered anyway. She agreed that I shouldn't, and that she'd been foolish to call me and I'd been less than wise to come running.

"But I'm glad you did," she said. "How long can you stay?"

"I've got return reservations in two and a half hours."

"So soon?"

"Uh-huh."

She sighed. "I wish you could stay longer. I know you can't. We don't even have time to—" She colored.

"We might have time," I said.

"I…I don't know. I'm not really in the mood, I don't think."

"It's a bad time for it."

"And a bad place. But God knows I need you, my darling—"

An invisible violinist played pizzicato on my vertebrae. I turned from her. "In Colorado," I said.

"Mmmmm. At Barnstable Lodge."

We'd taken to calling it that. "We should find a better name for it," I said.

"It's a fine name. Do you want coffee? I'll make some."

She went into the little kitchen to cook water. A fine domestic lady. I did not feel bad about the plane ride. It was nothing, just a little static, and worth a scare to see her, to be with her.

She called in: "I think I left my cigarettes on the table, John. Bring me one?"

I poked around in the pack. It was empty. I asked her if one of mine would do.

"Not really. I've got a fresh pack in my purse. I think it's in there somewhere. On the television, I think."

It was. I took it to her, opened the catch, fumbled inside for her cigarettes. She was at the stove spooning instant coffee into a pair of Melmac cups. All at once her eyes went very wide and her mouth shaped a small O. About that time my hand settled on something hard and cold. Some people could have guessed; I had to haul it out and look at it to know what it was.

It looked like a howitzer.

"Why?"

"I…oh, I don't even know. I've been dreaming about him, John. He'd kill me if he knew, I know he'd kill me, and I can't even think about it without turning cold inside. I thought it would be good to…to have something. In case something happened. I don't know."

"Where did you get it?"

"It's his."

"How come you've got it?"

"I took it. He kept it in his desk for years. Then it got switched to one of the filing cabinets. He'll never miss it. I don't think he's looked at it once in the past eight months."

"Ever shoot it?"

She shook her head.

"Ever handle *any* gun?"

"No."

"Then you probably couldn't do anything with it if you had to. Nine people out of ten can't hit the side of a garage at twenty feet with a handgun. The only time you might ever shoot this would be if you panicked. You would probably miss and be in deeper than ever. Or else you would kill somebody and get tagged with it.

"But chances are you'd never fire the gun at all. You'd just carry it, and you'd get unlucky and he'd just happen to look in your purse the way I just did. Or someone else would look in your purse, anyone. Or you'd drop the bag and the gun would go off. Or any of a thousand other damn fool things that wouldn't happen if you didn't do a harebrained thing and carry a gun along."

She stood wordless, and about to cry. The teakettle had been whistling throughout the tail end of my speech. I turned the burner off and the whistle died.

I said, "I didn't mean to fly at you like that. Guns make me as nervous as a virgin bride on opening night. They scare the hell out of me. I won't even work with anybody who carries one. All they buy you is trouble. A bank robber needs one, a killer needs one, all the thickheaded heavies need them. Nobody with a brain has to have a gun on his hip. Not even you."

"I feel—" I reached for her arm. She drew away. "I feel like an idiot," she said.

"Forget it. I'm just glad I found this thing."

"I almost wish you hadn't. You must think—"

"I think I'll be glad when this is over. And when you don't have to worry about anything more terrifying than what pattern glassware to buy for our little cabin in the pines. Is this loaded, by the way?"

"I think so."

I sat down on a kitchen chair, holding the gun gingerly. Guns do bother me. I hunted now and then when I was a kid, but nothing beyond birds and small game. I've never used a handgun. I do not like them at all. This one was a Smith and Wesson, .38-caliber, three-inch barrel, a safety on the grip. I shook my head at the last and thought she would never know to depress the grip safety before firing. The gun was all risk and no reward. I fumbled it open. It was loaded all the way, with a slug waiting there right smack under the hammer, which proved that Wally Gunderman didn't know a hell of a lot more about guns than she did.

I pulled its teeth, set the shells upright on the table top. I put the gun back together again and held it out toward her. She drew away and shook her head.

"I don't even want to touch it," she said.

"Should I leave it here? I could take it with me and dump it somewhere, but it would be better if you put it back in his files. If you'd rather not—"

"I don't mind. I just…put it on the counter, John. I don't want to touch it now. I'll take it with me when I go to work."

"I'll get rid of the shells for you."

"How?"

"I'll put them down a sewer. No problem."

"I'm nothing but problems tonight, aren't I?"

"I'm not complaining."

"Dragging you all the way here for nothing, and then this—"

"I'm glad I came. And glad I found out about the gun. It's worth the trip just keeping you from toting it around. You don't have to be scared of him, baby. He won't know a thing until you're a million miles away. He may never find out, he may drop dead long before he'd figure out that he's been had."

"It's this waiting—"

"You won't have to wait much longer."

We weren't any of us going to wait much longer. I had been laboring on details like Michelangelo on that Roman ceiling. I was so busy getting everything utterly perfect that I'd lost sight of a fairly important fact. Every extra day was just that much more hell for Evvie. I was hard at work on my masterpiece, and she was the one getting all that paint in her eyes. A bad mistake.

Not that day but the next I told Doug we were ready. And the following afternoon he called Gunderman and said yes to the deal, a firm yes, an all-the-way yes. An hour later I called Wally. Everything was set, he told me. In five days time he and Mr. Douglas Rance would put it all on paper. The deal was already being set up.

"I'll come in the night before," he told me. "You and I, John, we have some celebrating to do. You can show me that town and I'll teach you how to put a coat of paint on it."

I told him that sounded like a good idea.

So the days crawled by and the nights dawdled but passed, and he came to Toronto like Caesar to Rome. He wanted to hit every bar. We very nearly made it. He drank steadily and steadfastly refused to get bombed enough so that we could call it a day. I drank less than he did but not little enough to stay especially sober.

He did most of the talking. Some of it was about money, some of it was about Evvie. Once he gripped my arm and winked owlishly at me. "Some woman," he said. "Some wonderful woman."

I looked around to see who he meant. "Not *here*," he said. "I mean Evvie. One in a million."

"One in a million," I echoed. We were in complete agreement on that point.

He let go of my arm and dumped his face into one hand. He scratched idly at his earlobe. "If you only knew," he muttered secretly.

If *you* only knew, I thought.

And in some other remarkably similar bar he winked conspiratorially at me. I smiled politely and returned the wink, and he threw back his big head and roared.

"Easy," I said. The waiters were beginning to stare at us. "Easy, old pal."

"All mine," he said.

"Easy."

"Signed and sealed. All mine."

"All yours, old buddy. But take it easy."

He grabbed all the checks, overtipped all the waiters, winked at all the girls, and was the goddamned life of every goddamned party. "A celebration," he said, at least four hundred times. "A celebration."

I almost told him it was just a shade premature.

Back in my room, I was hanging my jacket over the back of a chair when the phone rang. I answered it, talked for a while. Then I got the rest of my clothes off and fell into bed, and the next thing I knew it was morning and the phone was ringing again.

Fifteen

Maybe I was getting old. When they rang the room in the morning the phone set little devils dancing in my head. I grabbed the phone and said all right, damn it, all right, and put the phone in the cradle and found my way to the john. The demons kept doing the twist inside my skull. I went through the standard wake-up ritual and tossed in a pair of aspirins and a Dexemil. All of this helped me wake up, and this in turn did little more than make me more aware of my headache. Too much Scotch, too little sleep—I was definitely getting too old for the life. The roadhouse in the mountains beckoned.

I put the good white shirt on once again, tied the small knot in the sincere tie, worked my way into the conservative suit. In another couple of hours I could unknot that tie and drop it in a handy wastebasket; in another couple of hours I could wipe the matching sincere look from my face and begin looking like me again. It was about time. The masquerade was beginning to make me ache, the costume was wearing thin on my frame. In another couple of hours—

Outside, the sun was all too bright. I let a couple of cups of coffee pretend to be breakfast and battled the sunlight once again. According to plans, I was supposed to be at the office at ten for the skinning ceremonies. It was time. I stepped to the curb, and a cab glided to me as if by magic. I hopped in and gave the driver the address.

It was funny. In the old days a time like this was always sweetly tense, the precious moment before the kill, the instant frozen in time when the matador stood poised, sword ready, with the great gross bull rushing in to impale himself and die in beauty. On mornings like this my eyes were bright and my head clear, and no quantity of liquor or shortness of sleep could cancel the fresh glory of it all.

It should have been like that now, and it was not. Not at all. Instead the hangover was in full bloom, aided and abetted by little grains of doubt and fear. Something gnawed at me. Something demanded attention. There was the feeling you get when you've left a room and you're dead certain you left a cigarette burning. Or the feeling you're left with after an alcoholic blackout—memory is gone, and you assume at once that you've done something dreadful; there are threads and patches in the back of your mind but not enough to grab onto and pin down, just enough to drive you mad.

"You're flipping," I said. "You're falling apart."

"What's that?"

This last from the cabby. I had been talking aloud and not realizing it, a phenomenon which is always less than comforting.

"Nothing," I said.

"You talking to me?"

"Just talking to myself."

"You always do that?"

"Just after a bad night."

"Oh," he said.

She'd be in Olean now, waiting. How long? A week for me to clear up everything in Toronto and get back to Colorado. A week was ample; our accounts had to be cleared, our front money had to be paid back, Gunderman's check had to be routed through channels. And it would be a week and more before she could pick up and join me. Call it ten days. In ten days we would be together, in Colorado, with all of his pretty money in our kick.

In ten days I could quit talking to myself.

Doug was already at the office, looking fresh and well-tailored. He looked at me and shuddered. "Bad?"

"You look like hell," he said.

"Well, he wanted to celebrate. We did most of the town."

"I thought you'd bring him with you. No?"

"He wanted to meet me here."

"At ten?"

"At ten."

"Fine," he said. "He should be here any minute. Everything's set, the papers, everything. That printer does choice work."

"He's expensive."

"Well, you get what you pay for, Johnny."

"That's if you're lucky."

"Sure." He walked around behind his desk, sat down, clasped his hands behind his neck, yawned, unclasped his hands and dug a cigarette out of his pack. He lit it and blew smoke at the ceiling. I looked at my watch. It was a few minutes past ten.

"Any minute, Johnny."

"Uh-huh."

"So smooth. I'm sorry you were stuck with him last night. He had big eyes to celebrate?"

"Bigger eyes than mine."

"I hope he didn't drink so much that he forgets to show up. It's been so damned smooth so far. Like silk. Was he holding it pretty well?"

"Better than I was."

"You didn't let anything out?"

I gave him a look.

"Well, forget I asked."

I took a cigarette, lit it. The gnawing inside wouldn't go away. I told Doug that Gunderman should be here by now. "He doesn't get places late," I said. "He's always on time. It's one of his virtues."

"Maybe he wants to play hard to get."

"Isn't it a little late for that? You don't walk around with your skirt around your waist for a month and then play hard to get when you finally work your way to the bedroom. He should have been here with bells on. He should have been here before I was, for Christ's sake."

"You're getting a little jumpy, Johnny."

He was right. I was getting more than a little jumpy, and I liked it less and less. I do not like it when people act out of character. I do not like it when patterns are broken. And I like it least of all toward the end of the game, when it is either in or out and no mending the fences once they break. Things can be shaky in the early stages. You aren't committed, nobody is committed, and you can all feel your way, and back and fill to make things right. But there is no backing or filling as you approach the wire. It has to be perfect, clean and sweet, and any deviations from the norm do not sit well with me.

"Sit down, Johnny." I hadn't even realized I was pacing. I went on pacing. "Sit down, damn it, you're making me nervous." He stubbed out his cigarette. "You know what's the matter with you?"

"What?"

"You're losing your goddamned nerve. A few years in San Quentin and you get shaky in the clinches. Johnny, you couldn't ask for a smoother job than this. Will you sit down and relax?"

I looked at my watch. "No," I said, "I won't."

"What are you doing?"

"Calling him," I said.

I grabbed the phone and rang the Royal York. The desk man was a long time answering. I asked him if Mr. Gunderman was in, not to bother him but to see if his key was there. He took his time and then told me no, the key was not in the box.

"Ring his room," I said.

Doug told me I was crazy. I waved him off. The clerk plugged me in and let the phone ring. He let it ring a long time. Nobody answered that phone.

"Shall I check his room, sir?"

I looked down at my hand. The fingers were trembling slightly all by themselves. "No, don't do that," I said steadily. "He must have left and taken his key with him. It's perfectly all right."

The clerk didn't pursue the subject. I thanked him, and he rang off.

I said, "No answer. He didn't leave and he doesn't answer. He always gets places on time and he's not here yet."

"Johnny—"

"Come on, will you?"

"Where?"

"His hotel."

He looked at me as if he was measuring me for a straitjacket. "He's on his way over here, Johnny," he said levelly. "Now calm down, will you? He took his key with him, the way you told it to the clerk, and in one minute he's going to walk through that door, and—"

I took him by the arm and yanked. "You can wait until hell's six feet deep in snow," I said. "He's never coming through that door."

"Johnny—"

"And we're going over there. And fast."

"Johnny." He drew himself up straight. He was trying not to look at all nervous, and he was almost making it. "This is my set-up," he said. "I'm not letting you blow it."

"It's blown to hell and back," I told him. "Move."

Our cab seemed to crawl. The traffic was thick and the driver less than aggressive. We filled the back of the cab with cigarette smoke and the odor of coolish sweat. All the way there I had the very bad feeling that I had somehow dreamed this entire scene before. Sometime in the depth of sleep I had lived through this episode, and in the morning the memory was gone like smoke. Once I had dreamed this, and I should have remembered the dream. It would have made things much simpler.

When the cab stopped I threw a five at the driver and did not wait for change. On the way into the lobby I told Doug to follow me and not say anything or do anything spectacular. "We are not stopping at the desk," I told him. "We are going straight to his room. I know where it is."

He didn't answer. He had lost the sense of the play. He knew only that something was very wrong, and that I was probably out of my mind, and that it was easier to go along with me than to make me listen to reason. I got us to the elevator and rode one floor above his. I got us out of the elevator, and we went down the stairs to the right floor and along the corridor to his room.

Doug said, "I don't get it."

"You will."

"He's probably at the office right now. Or he's

sleeping; he got bombed last night and he's sleeping it off."

"If he's at the office he can wait for us," I said. "If he's bombed, we'll apologize for interrupting him. We'll say we were worried about him, that we wanted to check."

"I still say this is stupid."

"You don't know what stupid is," I said.

I knocked heavily on Gunderman's door. One thoroughly wishful corner of my mind expected him to lumber to the door and open it. I did not really expect this, and I was not at all surprised when it did not happen. I reached into my hip pocket and got out my wallet. I took out a gas company credit card.

"Johnny—"

"Shut up."

The corridor was empty. I worked the credit card between the door and the jamb, and Doug nudged me, and I withdrew the card and waited for a man with an attaché case to emerge from a room down the hall and make his way past us to the elevators. When he was gone I wedged the credit card back where it belonged.

Hotel room locks are nothing at all, not in the fleabags, not in the good places either. I popped the bolt back and turned the knob and pushed the door open.

"If he's in there—"

If he was, he hadn't bolted the door. You can't snick back the inside bolt that way. You only get the one that spring-locks the door from the outside.

I pushed the door open. I went inside, and Doug came after me, and I remembered to shut the door after us. We went inside, and there was the bed and the chair and the dresser and some clothes scattered, and there was what I had somehow known we would find. Because I must have dreamed it all one night, dreamed it and forgotten it somewhere in the dark places of the night.

There was Gunderman, sprawled on the floor between the bed and the wall. He was in his pajamas, loud blue cotton pajamas. He had been shot twice at fairly close range. There were two holes in his chest, quite close together, and one of them must have placed itself in his heart because there was not much blood around. Almost all of it was on his pajamas, with just a little soaking into the rug.

Doug was making meaningless sounds beside me. I looked back stupidly to make sure that the door was closed. It was. I looked around the room. The gun was not too far from the body. I went over to all that was left of our pigeon and knelt down beside him. I touched the side of his face. His flesh was cool but not cold, and the bits of blood were drying but not yet dry. Someone with a better background than mine could have said with assurance just how long dead he was. It was out of my line. I never had all that much to do with dead men.

"Oh, Johnny—"

I walked over to where the gun lay. A good manly gun. Guns were not my line either, but I knew the make and model of this one. A .38 Smith and Wesson with a three-inch barrel and a safety on the grip. I knew it well.

"Don't touch it, Johnny."

I picked up the gun.

"Brilliant," he was saying. "Oh, brilliant. Now you've got your prints all over the damned thing, Johnny."

I knew better. They were already there. I'd put them there long ago in another town in another country. *Get me one of my cigarettes, John*—and that gun in her purse, waiting to be found, waiting to be gripped. She'd never touched it after that. She let me unload it and put it away myself. She never laid a finger on it—until later, alone, with gloves on, once to load it and once this morning to fire it, twice. I looked down at that dead man and envied him.

Sixteen

"She killed him," I said. I was a little shaky and my eyes weren't focusing properly. "This...I put my prints on this gun a week ago. It was her gun, she conned me into picking it up and playing with it."

"Where did you see her?"

"Olean. She—"

"You took a trip a week ago? You didn't tell me."

"She was—" the words came slow, "nervous, she said. She thought things were falling in. It turned out to be a false alarm, but in the middle of it she set me up to find the gun for her."

"You never said a thing." His tone was flat, hard.

"She didn't want me to."

"She *what*?"

"I was hung on the girl," I said.

"Give me that again."

I turned on him. "I was in love with the bitch," I said, "and I was taken. But how the hell did she get here? I talked to her last night. She called me last night, dammit, and she called long-distance. I don't get any of this."

"Oh, Christ."

"What?"

"I thought she was calling Gunderman."

I grabbed his arm. "Give me that again. From the beginning."

It was his turn to look worried. "She flew into town yesterday afternoon," he said. "So she would be here after the job was over."

"After the job—"

"We were going to fly to Vegas. The two of us." I did not say anything. "Well, she's a good piece, damn it. She didn't want you to know because she said you tried and struck out."

"I got the same line."

"You're kidding."

"The hell I am. What kind of a damn fool are you, flying her to Toronto? What's the brilliant point of that?"

"Johnny—"

"I talked to her last night. First an operator, person-to-person, and then—"

He was just shaking his head. "I thought it was Gunderman, Johnny. Oh, Jesus. She said she wanted to call Gunderman and make it seem like a long-distance call. I sat right there in the room with her. I told her how to fake the operator's voice. She held a handkerchief over the phone and talked very distinctly and a little nasally with the phone about six inches from her mouth. And then took the handkerchief off and got close to the phone when she was playing Evvie again. Oh, she is cute."

"Yeah."

"And I sat there in the room and thought she was talking to him."

She was very cute. I thought back to the conversation, trying to remember. "She asked for me," I said. "By name. Were you in the room when she played the operator bit?"

"I must have been."

"Then—"

"No, she wanted a drink. I went into the kitchen. I thought I heard—oh, damn it."

I'd admired her timing before. The slipped kiss in front of his office building, the sweet way she had of playing things like a true-blooded professional. And I had thought she was only playing one side. She'd played all three of us, and played us off the wall.

She had never mentioned my name. And she had thrown me a conversation that she could as well have thrown to Gunderman. How she missed me, and how she hoped everything would go all right, and how she couldn't wait to see me again. I remembered now that she had sounded a little less hip than usual. No grifter argot. It wouldn't have done the necessary double duty. She never missed a trick.

"Johnny, if you had *said* something—"

"Me?"

"You said she didn't mean a thing to you. If I knew she did I would have seen her angle. You blew this one, Johnny."

I forced myself to stay steady. "You're a pretty one," I said. "You're so in love with yourself you can't see straight. You're so damned busy being the hottest puff of smoke since the Yellow Kid. You put this on the screw from the beginning."

"How?"

"You balled her in Vegas, didn't you?"

He told me so with his eyes.

"You should have said it then. You should have let this thing play straight from the beginning, but you had to be goddamned cute about it. I'd like a chance at you, Rance."

"Any time."

I almost swung. I don't know what stopped me, but I almost swung, and that would have torn it for good. It's not a good idea to start a fight and draw a crowd, not when you've got a corpse on the floor and the murder gun carries your prints.

I looked at him and said, "Later."

"All right."

"We've got to dig out from under."

"Pick up the gun and leave."

He was full of bright ideas. I told him how far we'd get. We were tied to Gunderman a hundred different ways. There were too many papers in his office with our names on them, too many connections. This had to be staged just as neatly as any blow-off operation. We were blowing off a dead man instead of a live one. That was the only difference. It took just as sure a touch, just as firm a sense of the game.

It took two cigarettes. Then I had it. I said, "There's a way. You'll need a suitcase. And a wallet with fake identification."

"I've got both at the apartment."

"Good. You leave the hotel now. Go out a back entrance, grab a cab, go to your place." I went over to the window. "I hope your fake ID sets you up in some far-away place."

"I've got papers for California. Los Angeles, I think."

"Good. Throw a few things in a suitcase. California labels, nothing else. You're close enough to his size to do it. Then get in another cab and come back to the hotel. Go to the desk and check in under the phony name. Get a room as close to this one as you can. The same side of the building. Tell them you want to face whatever the hell that street is out there. One floor away is fine. One floor away is better than the same floor, actually. You with me?"

"I guess so."

"Check in, go to your room, and then get back here. I'll have it set up. We've got a few things going for us. He checked in yesterday afternoon. The kid on the desk now never saw him, not yesterday afternoon and not last night. We've just about got time. Move."

"Johnny?"

"What?"

"I can't figure the cross. He had the money with him. It might still be around—"

"It won't be. She took it."

"Even so. She gets seventy thou instead of seven-teen-five. She doesn't figure to kill for the difference, does she?"

"I'll tell you later," I said.

When he left I shut the door and bolted it after him. I did not want any hyperefficient maid stumbling in on me. Then I walked into the john and washed my hands and dried them on a towel and went back to get things in motion. I found his suitcase on the floor of the closet. I packed his clothes in it. I went through the dresser and the pockets of his clothes and picked off everything that gave a clue as to who he was and where he came from. All of this went into the suitcase. I got his money belt—you don't see them much any more, but he'd had one and she would have known about it. I wasn't surprised to find it empty.

There was a cashier's check in his wallet, drawn to the order of the Barnstable Corporation and made out in the amount of forty thousand dollars. I tucked this in my own wallet, then thought a moment and switched his wallet for my own. If I was going to be him I might as well do it right.

When I first started to move him, I thought I might be sick. I got past the first rush of nausea and then things settled down. He wasn't a corpse, he was just a dead weight. I dragged him a few feet away and checked the carpet where he had lain.

It wasn't bad. Not too much blood, really, and the

carpet was nylon and not especially absorbent. I wetted some toilet paper and wiped it so that it looked clean. Spectroscopic analysis would show blood for weeks, but if things broke right nobody would come looking, and if things went wrong they wouldn't need bloodstains to hang us.

I tried to keep busy that way. As long as I was doing things, moving and staying active, I didn't have to think so hard about things that were better unexamined. Like the sweet way she'd set it up. Like the reason she worked the cross.

She hadn't killed him for the simple arithmetical difference between seventeen and seventy thousand dollars. She had killed him for the whole bundle. She wanted everything, everything that belonged to Wallace J. Gunderman.

She'd get it, too. Because the bitch had married him.

I lit a cigarette. He'd as much as told me the night before, and I had been too damned stupid to pick it up then and there. All of that coyness—I'd taken it for granted he was acting that way because he thought I was hung on Evvie while he was actually keeping her and using her to keep me on his team. But the words he'd used made more sense now. He had *married* her.

It made more sense that way.

And other parts made sense. The attitude he'd shown all those times pointed out one thing—since his wife died, he had been the one pushing for marriage and she had been busy putting him off. It added up a million times as sensibly that way. She had waited, and she had finally gone and married him just in time to be his widow.

What was he worth? A few million? And to that you could tack on a whole load of extras, like the hate she had for him and the kick she must have felt when the gun went off. It all tallied out to a lot more than the seventeen and a half thousand dollars that she was supposed to get out of the deal. It added up to many miles more than a roadhouse in Colorado and a broken-down grifter for a husband and "Hearts and Flowers" for a theme song.

We were supposed to get stuck with it. We'd be tied up tight, and she could keep herself in the clear. She had never put anything on paper. We could never drag her into it. We could only tighten the noose around our own necks.

I lit another cigarette and wished to hell Doug would get back. We had a chance, I thought. Getting to his hotel room on time had opened it up for us. And Doug was about his build—that helped. And the timing with the hotel clerks. We did not exactly have the odds on our side, and if we had held those cards in a poker game I would have thrown our hand in and folded. But you can't ever fold when your whole damned life's in the pot. You have to play whatever's dealt.

He knocked on the door and said, "Doug here," his voice pitched low and tense. I opened the door. He was wearing a hat and he had a cigar in his mouth. He came inside and drew the door shut.

"He's going to be me," he said. "Right?"

"That's the idea."

"That's why the cigar and the hat, and why I acted middle-aged for the clerk. Gunderman does smoke cigars, doesn't he?"

"Not any more."

"I guess not. The money was gone?"

"All but the check. That was there. To lead them to us fast, I suppose."

He shook his head. "I'd love to kill that girl."

"You'd have to stand in line. Where's your room?"

It was one flight downstairs. That made it a little easier. We slipped Gunderman out of his pajamas and put a suit of Doug's on him—dressing a dead man is every bit as unpleasant as it sounds. The shoes and socks were the hardest part. When we were done with him he wouldn't have stood inspection, but then he probably wouldn't have to. The hotel was fairly empty at that hour, and most people don't pay any particular attention to things that don't involve them.

At least that's what we told ourselves. It's not easy to work yourself up to the point where you can cart a corpse around a hotel without losing your air of nonchalance.

Doug checked the corridor. We waited until it was empty, at least on our floor. Then we hoisted him up and each of us draped one of his dead arms over our shoulders. He was supposed to look drunk, or sick, or something, and we were his good friends helping poor Clyde back to his room. This was the script. It wouldn't win Oscars, but it had to do the job.

He was very damned heavy, even with the load shared between us. We got him out into the hallway. I kicked the door shut, and we headed for the stairs. As we got there I heard an elevator coming. We ducked into the stairwell just as the door opened on our floor. Whoever got off, we weren't spotted.

The stairs were easy. We got down them in a hurry, and I stood at the landing with Gunderman draped all over me while Doug checked the traffic on the floor. There was a maid en route, her cart of clean linen blocking our way. We waited for her, and she took her time, until finally she busied herself in one of the bathrooms. She couldn't see the hallway from there. Doug grabbed hold of Gunderman and we took him for another walk. We couldn't rush, because the whole scene had to look natural if anyone happened to glance our way.

No one did. We made it to the room and closed the damned door and eased our plucked pigeon down onto the floor. I wanted a cigarette. Instead I lit one of Gunderman's cigars, and so did Doug. We put another one in the pocket of Doug's suit.

The rest was frosting. We unpacked Doug's suitcase and put his clothes away in the dresser and in the closet. With the end of my cigar, I burned a pair of holes in Gunderman's shirt right above the bullet holes. They did not look exactly like .38-caliber powder burns but they were close enough for the time being.

We planted the fake wallet in his pocket, tossed Doug's hat on his dresser, dropped our cigar butts in the ashtrays. Then for a finale, we tucked Gunderman in the closet and closed the door on him.

If the bitch had only shot him once, we could have staged it as suicide. But nobody shoots himself twice in the chest. It was as well to make it a murder and let them figure out why and by whom. We left him in the closet and went back to Gunderman's room.

"Don't get noticed on the way out," I said.

"Right."

"I'll catch you at the office."

"Right."

I gave him a few minutes. Then I hefted a bag with W.J.G. properly embossed upon it, lifted the phone, told the desk to get my bill ready. They said they would. I gave the room a last check, left it, went to the elevator and rode down to the lobby. I should have been nervous. I wasn't, for some odd reason. Everything was crystal clear now. All I had to do was go by the book. I was Wallace J. Gunderman, and I was checking out of their hotel, and once I was gone they could put me out of their minds forever. They would never fasten my name onto the dead thing a floor away.

I gave the room key to the clerk. He looked up at me brightly. "You had a call about an hour ago, Mr. Gunderman—"

"I know, I was in the shower. Any message?"

"No, he didn't leave his name."

"Well, I think I know who it was. No problem."

He had my bill ready. While I checked it over he asked me if I had enjoyed my stay. I said I had. With phone calls and room service the tab came to a little short of twenty bucks. I put Gunderman's Diners Club card on the counter, then snatched it back just as the clerk was reaching for it. I wanted to flash it but I didn't want to risk a phony signature on the hotel books.

"Let me pay cash," I said. "I don't want to mix them up with charges in Canadian funds."

He couldn't argue with logic like that. I gave him a twenty, and he gave me change and stamped my bill and handed it to me. I stuck it in Gunderman's wallet and stuck the wallet in my pocket and picked up my suitcase and headed for the door. Nobody stopped me.

Seventeen

Doug had a few things to do. He had to clear out his apartment, and he had to turn the Barnstable offices into a ghost town. We were on too many official records and we had scattered too much correspondence to strike our sets completely, but Doug could wipe out some of the more obvious traces. This is easy when you have all the time in the world. We had to move fast, and we had to do what we could.

But that was a minor headache. The important thing was something else again. We had two definite facts to contend with—there was a dead man in a closet in the Royal York, and there was a man named Wallace J. Gunderman who had disappeared. If anybody matched the name and the body, then we were in trouble. The longer it took them to put the two together, the better off we were. We had given the body a name and a logical way of dying. Now we had to take the Gunderman identity and find a way to let it trail off and dissolve like smoke.

He had return reservations to Olean for the late afternoon. I called the airport and changed his reservations, asking them for the first plane to Chicago.

They had a flight at three-fifteen. I booked a seat on the plane in Gunderman's name.

Doug was waiting for me at the office. He had called Helen Wyatt to tell her that things had gone sour, and that she should let the other hired hands know as much. They didn't stand any chance of getting involved—Gunderman alone had seen them, and he wasn't going to tell anyone—and by the same token they weren't likely to involve us. It was a courtesy call. When the ship sinks, a good captain at least lets the crew know about it.

"I'm packed and ready," he said. "Got any cash?"

"A couple of hundred. You?"

"A little more. And there's a little over twelve thou in the bank, the Barnstable account. If we can get it."

"No problem there. A day or two from now it might be tight, but nobody's going to put a freeze on our account for the time being."

He whistled soundlessly. "We can't get rich this way. Anyway, it's a stake. I'm out a few thou but not as much as I expected."

"You're forgetting something."

"What?"

"Terry Moscato."

His face fell. "That's ten grand."

"Plus interest. Eleven thousand. That leaves us with cabfare."

"We can't pay him."

"We damn well have to. You don't cross the man

who bankrolls you. That's one thing you don't do. You can lie to your partner—"

"I'm not the only one, Johnny."

"All right. Put a lid on it. You don't stiff Moscato, not because it's a case of honor among thieves but because you'd wind up dead. I mean it. He's the easiest man to work with as long as you're good, but if you play him bad you've had it. He is hard."

"Eleven thousand dollars."

"We've got twelve or so in the bank. And I'm holding Gunderman's check for forty more."

He'd forgotten about it. This was easy to do. We'd been crossed and skinned and sliced up for bait, and it was hard to regard that cashier's check as anything more than a prop she'd left for the police to play with. Besides, it was a dead man's check. A dead man's check is not negotiable. It's evidence of a receivable asset, and you can hold it as a claim against the estate of the deceased, but you cannot scrawl your name across the back of it and pass it to a friendly neighborhood teller. It's locked up tight. Our check was signed by Gunderman, and he was as dead as you can get.

"But nobody knows this," I said. "It's going to be a long time before they know he's dead. We can get rid of the paper long before then."

"Discount it and sell it?"

"I think it's easier to cash it. Just shove it the hell through the Barnstable account."

"And when that check works its way back to his bank?"

"That's days from now. And who's going to look at it, anyway?" I crushed a cigarette in the ashtray. "There's a big unknown here. I'm not sure how she's going to play it. Right now she's sure we're going to get picked up for this one by nightfall. She left a deep wide trail and it leads straight to us and she'll be expecting a call sometime this evening telling her that her husband is dead."

"That's the part I can't believe."

"That he married her?"

"Yeah."

I made him believe it. Then I carried it further. She'd be waiting for that call, and by early evening she'd be starting to sweat. Cool or not, the act of killing was going to get to her sooner or later. And when she had time to think about it, she couldn't miss seeing that it would be tough for her to keep her fingers clean once they picked us up and we talked.

Because we would have to talk, and we would have to sing out her name loud and clear. We might not be able to prove it. If we did, we were still up to our ears in it; as parties to the con game felony we were legally parties to the murder, like it or not. So we were in trouble, but she was going to have some of it rub off on her. She might not do a bit for murder, might not serve any time at all, but she would have it much easier if we escaped free and clear, and she couldn't help figuring that out in time.

All of this left her a handy out. She could sit on her hands for a while, saying that Gunderman had gone off on a business trip and she didn't know when he would be back. Finally she could report him missing, but by this time she could have all the Barnstable correspondence cleared from his files. If our cashier's check cleared his bank, she could head it off and get rid of it.

They might make the murder connection after a while, but we'd be light years away by then and she wouldn't steer them toward us. They might not pin the Gunderman label on the Royal York corpse at all. We were trailing Gunderman to Chicago and losing him there. And good hotels don't publicize men who get murdered on the premises. It's bad for business. The Royal York would keep the newspaper publicity to a minimum on their dead man. Gunderman might wind up permanently missing. Evvie would have enough control of his money to live it up for the seven years it would take to declare him legally dead. Then she could take the whole bundle.

She might not like it that way, but she could drift into the pattern very easily. As the wife of a missing man, she could live as lush a life as ever. She didn't have to stay in Olean.

And once the seven years played themselves out she was home free.

The bitch didn't have it so bad. She'd spend seven years waiting for an Enoch Arden decree, and they'd go a lot faster and pass a lot more pleasantly than the seven years I had done in Q. When they ran out, she'd pick up the pot of gold. All I'd landed was a brass check and a night-man slot at a bowling alley.

When I ran out of words we stood there smoking and listening to the silence. He broke it first. "We can come out clean," he said, and his voice turned it into a prayer.

"Maybe. And probably not. If I had to lay odds I'd guess that they'll tag us for murder inside of a month and spend three months trying to find us before they write us off. Our prints are on file, but that doesn't matter if we never get mugged and printed. We'll be across a national border. We'll have different names and different haircuts. I think we ought to make it, but we won't come up smelling of roses."

He thought it over. I thought about that warm woman and how well I'd been had. I had never felt so much like a mooch. The depths of her eyes, the little sounds of liquid desperation she made in bed. It was hard to believe that all of these things could have been counterfeit.

Forget it. It was every mark's story, in technicolor on a wide wide screen with a cast of thousands. *He was such a nice man, Mommy. I can't believe such a nice man would steal my candy. He seemed so sincere, Mommy—*

Forget it.

I went to our bank and deposited Gunderman's check to our account. I let the same teller handle a withdrawal for me, and I took an even twenty thousand dollars in cash. This didn't throw her. The cashier's check was as good as gold, and I could have tried to get the full amount in cash if I had wanted to. I didn't. I took the twenty thou from the one girl, and I had another girl certify a check for thirty-one thousand dollars payable to P. T. Parker in U.S. funds. I went to my other bank where I had the Parker account, deposited this check and bought five bank drafts payable to cash for varying amounts ranging from five to ten thousand dollars each.

In a third bank, I used the Canadian cash to buy a few more bank drafts and a handful of traveler's cheques. I held out eleven thousand in U.S. dollars. In the main post office, I packed away the bank drafts in individual envelopes and mailed them off. I shipped a few of them to Robert W. Pattison at the Hotel Mark Twain in Omaha. I scattered the rest around the Midwest, mostly in Kansas and Iowa, sending them to various names at various general delivery offices. I mailed a little less than half of them from the Toronto Post Office and kept the rest aside.

There was just enough time for a telephone call before my plane was ready to go. It took a few tries to reach Terry Moscato. I finally got him.

I said, "I think you know me. Can you talk now?"

"I know you, and I can talk, but no names or details. Go ahead."

"It's done. It went to hell, but it's done. I have the goods you want and I'd like to deliver."

"I'd be glad to have you make delivery. Are you sure you've got the right size?"

"Size eleven," I said.

"That's fine. Can you come to town for delivery?"

"Not very easily."

"If I arranged a pick-up," he said carefully, "there would be an additional handling charge."

I didn't want him to send a boy, handling charge or no. "I was thinking about the mails," I said.

"I don't like that."

"Not from this port. A standard interstate shipment, registered and insured."

The line was silent while he thought this over. There is nothing safer than registered and insured mail. But he still didn't like it.

"Railway Express," he said.

"Seriously?"

"Definitely. The same drop." And he rang off. I wondered what he had against the mails.

They were already calling my flight when I remembered two things. The gun and the money. I had the murder gun and a pair of bloody pajamas in my suitcase, and I had eleven thousand dollars of Moscato's money keeping them company.

On an ordinary flight this wouldn't have mattered. It's against some silly law to carry a gun on a plane, but no one normally paws through your baggage or frisks you as you enter the plane. This was not an entirely normal flight. This was a flight from one country to another, and that meant going through Customs. You lose sight of this when the two countries are the States and Canada. Customs inspections are cursory at best—every fifth car going over a bridge, a quick peek in suitcases on a plane ride. If your contraband is something as innocuous as a fifth of undeclared Scotch, you don't break out in a rash worrying about getting tagged. When you're packing eleven thousand dollars that you can't explain along with a gun that's just been used in a murder, it gets a little sticky.

There was no place to stash the gun, no handy way to conceal the dough. I ducked into the men's room and got the suitcase open. I ripped the pajamas apart, flushed the singed and bloody pieces down the toilet along with the Olean label and tucked the rest in the trashcan. I parceled up the stack of hundred-dollar bills. There were a hundred and ten of them, and by balancing them off in various pockets and lodging a healthy sheaf of them in my wallet, I managed to spread them over my person without bulging anywhere.

That left the gun. And I didn't dare dump it anywhere in Canada, because a ballistics check would tie it to the dead man in the closet, and this would not be good at all. I couldn't know where she bought the gun. It might have come out of Olean originally, and that was the sort of link I did not want to supply. Ideally the gun would be broken down and spread out over a score of sewer systems. In a pinch it would be wiped free of prints inside and out and dropped into a river a thousand miles away from Toronto. But it couldn't stay in the city, and it couldn't ride on my person, and it could not nestle in my suitcase.

They called the flight again. I couldn't miss it or they would start paging Wallace J. Gunderman over the P.A. system. This was not precisely what I had in mind. The Customs inspection wouldn't come now, at least. It would come when we got to O'Hare. I could sneak the gun onto the plane. But I couldn't take it off or leave it behind.

Beautiful. I wedged it into a pocket. It looked as inconspicuous as an albino in Harlem. I grabbed my suitcase and ran for the plane.

The plane was mostly full. I had an aisle seat just forward of the wing. My seat partner was a youngish woman with a sharp nose and acne scars. She read a Canadian magazine and ignored me entirely. I fastened my belt and put out my cigarette and told the stewardess that I did not want a magazine, and we left the ground and aimed at Chicago.

The .38 was burning a hole in my pocket. There were any number of ways to get rid of it and none of them looked especially attractive. I could stow it under a seat, set it on top of the luggage rack, even make a stab at dumping it into somebody's suitcase. Whatever I did, it was an odds-on bet that the gun would turn up within an hour after landing, and probably before then. I took a hike to the john, and that was no help at all. Just the bare essentials. No handy hiding place for a hunk of steel that was hotter than…well, hotter than a pistol.

I tried to think it through and couldn't get anywhere. I kept coming back to the job itself, how smoothly it had gone, how thoroughly it had gone to hell for itself. I was a long time hating a girl named Evelyn Stone. I thought about a hundred different ways to make her dead and couldn't find one mean enough for her. She had conned me as utterly as a man can be conned. She had not merely made me trust her. She had made me love her, and then she stuck it in and broke it off deep.

A funny thing. I wanted badly to hate her, but I kept losing my grip and easing up on all of that hate. I couldn't hold onto it. She had not betrayed any love because she had faked and manipulated that crock of love from the beginning. Ever since she first latched onto Doug in Vegas, long before she ever set eyes on me, I was her pigeon. She never owed me a thing. If I had seen her within the first couple of hours after we found Gunderman's body, I probably would have killed her. The rage was fresh then. Time took the edge off it in a hurry. I couldn't even summon up any really strong craving for revenge. I might never be a charter member of her fan club, but the real gut-bucket hate was gone.

Evelyn Stone had played our little game according to the rules; it was only sad that she and I had been on opposite sides, and that I had not known this. But there was one person who had broken the rules. Right at the start he forgot the one cardinal injunction. Never, under any circumstances, do you play fast and loose with your partner.

Doug crossed me from the opening whistle. He must have known all along that I had a weakness for women, an irritating habit of going overboard for them. So he didn't bother telling me that he'd pushed Evvie over on her round little heels. That set everything in motion. Once he established the pattern, she played us off so neatly that we never felt the strings. He had not meant to mess me up. It was just the way he chose to run his show. It had to be his show all the way—his ego wouldn't let go of it—and that made him improvise, keeping part of the picture hidden, keeping me just far enough in the dark so that things had a chance to go to hell for themselves.

You don't do that to your partner. That's the one thing you don't do, and he'd done it and set Evvie up so that I wound up doing the same thing. And if I didn't hate her any more, that didn't mean I was in love with the whole world and at peace with mankind. Not at all.

The sharp-nosed girl beside me stirred in her seat. Down the aisle, the stewardess began serving the meal, the usual airline fare, as sterile and tasteless as the stewardess herself. I broke off my woolgathering and thought about the gun.

There's always a way. I let the girl serve me my dinner. I ate about half of it and drank a cup of luke-warm coffee. When she took my tray away, my knife wasn't on it. It was on my lap.

I reached down between my knees and worked on the front edge of my seat with the knife. It was a steak knife, sharp enough on the edge of the blade but not too keen at the tip, and this made it slow going. Once I broke through the vinyl it got easier. I had to keep stopping; the stewardess was walking back and forth, as busy as a speakeasy on Election Day, and my seat-mate had turned restless and was given to looking my way. But before too long I had a good hiding place arranged, with the slit just wide enough to admit the gun but small enough to retain it and to pass unnoticed for a good long time.

I couldn't think of a clever way to pull the gun out of my hip pocket without attracting attention. Finally I went to the john again and came out with the gun wrapped in a paper towel. I sat down again, and when the opportunity came I slipped the gun out of its paper envelope and wedged it into the seat. Someday someone would find it there and wonder how in hell it got there. But they would have no idea what passenger on what flight put it there, and by then it wouldn't · matter any more.

We landed five minutes ahead of schedule at O'Hare. The Customs man asked me if I had anything to declare, and I said I hadn't. He asked me how long I had been in Canada. I told him something. He opened my suitcase but didn't do more than glance in it before passing me on. I could have had three pounds of heroin and an M-l rifle in there and he never would have noticed it.

I stayed at the terminal long enough to practice Gunderman's signature, copying it from his driver's license and a few other cards in his wallet. I'm fair but not perfect with a pen. I would never fool an expert, but I might not have to. I would sign his name once, on the hotel registration card, and that would be all. If I could come fairly close, that would probably be good enough.

I cabbed to the Palmer House. They had a single available and I took it. I signed in, did a fair job with the signature, and went to my room. I had a couple of things to do in Chicago and more than enough time to do them.

I packed eleven thousand dollars in a cigar box and packaged it with tender loving care. At the Railway Express office, I shipped it to Terry Moscato's address and insured it, appropriately enough, for eleven thousand dollars. I told the clerk the parcel contained jewelry. He could not have cared less.

On the way back I called the Palmer House and asked for myself. They rang my room and told me that I wasn't there. I thanked them. I went to the hotel and the clerk told me there had been a call for me, and gave me the message I had left. I thanked him and went to the room to pick up the envelopes from the suitcase, a handful of bank drafts to be mailed to different places. I bought stamps from a machine in the lobby and mailed them. I went to a movie house on South Dearborn and sat through most of a double feature. I had dinner across the street from the theater and decided to use Gunderman's credit card and sign his name a second time. I did an even better job with the signature this time around.

The rest was just putting in time. I hit a couple of bars and sorted things out in my mind. By now Doug was probably in Omaha, waiting for me. I'd get there in time to help him pick up the bank drafts that I was scattering all over the Midwest. I tried to figure out just how much cash I was going to realize on the deal. We'd wind up holding something like forty thou, give or take a little, and Doug would draw ten off the top, the original working capital that he'd contributed. The rest would get cut up straight down the middle. No matter how you counted, that made my end in the neighborhood of fifteen grand.

I had another beer and thought about it. It wasn't all that bad. Getting anything at all was a fluke—hell, beating the murder rap was a fluke, as far as that went.

Fifteen thousand dollars. It was possible. Bannion could give a certain amount of ground; if I played him right, I could get his place for less than I'd figured, and if I couldn't find the right pitch to hand that old lush I might as well call it a day. If I arranged the right sort of financing and played it close to the vest for the first two or three years, I just might manage to handle the deal after all. It would be close, but it might work.

Ideally, I should have more money to play with. But dreams rarely come true, and never materialize without losing a certain amount of their glow. The original dream sparkled like diamonds—plenty of money and a girl to make it all worthwhile. If I could just squeeze by I was still coming out with a rosy smell.

I called the hotel again and found another bar to

play in. It turned out to be a long night. Somewhere toward the tail end of it I spent enough time in a joint on North Clark to pick up a semi-pro hooker with oversized breasts and too much makeup. We went to her place and made a brave try, but I couldn't do anything. This didn't come as much of a surprise. I may have stopped hating her, but I hadn't yet lost the taste of her. That would take a while.

Eighteen

I don't know whether they can handle jets at Omaha or not. The plane I took was a prop job, an old DC-7. It got me there fast enough. I'd stayed two nights and a day at the Palmer House before making reservations from Chicago to Buffalo in Gunderman's name. He'd never make that flight, but it could let them think he'd headed back toward Olean, or planned on it, before something went haywire. If they traced it that far. It was mostly just a question of going through the motions, setting up a few false trails partly for insurance and partly for practice. I'd made the reservation, and then I went out to O'Hare and caught a plane, not for Buffalo but for Omaha. I left his suitcase and his clothes in the room. I took the wallet with me, because men do not leave their wallets in their hotel rooms. In the can at O'Hare I burned up what cards and papers he had that would burn, dropped them in the bowl and flushed them away. The wallet was anonymous enough to go in the wastebasket. The various credit cards would neither burn nor flush nor disappear. I bought a small packet of razor blades at the newsstand and used one of them to slice the cards into strips. I threw the strips away and threw the blades away and waited for my plane. I had a few things in a canvas flight bag. The rest of my clothes were in Omaha. I was anxious to get to them. Gunderman's clothes did not fit me, and I'd been wearing one change of clothing for too many days.

The airport was thick with police. A day ago they'd have bothered me. Now I hardly noticed them.

The tension was wearing away. A couple of days ago we had been inches from the pot of gold at the rainbow's end, and my skin had been too tight over my bones and sweat came freely. Then in a few fast minutes the gold faded out and there was nothing but a noose at the end of that rainbow. It got very tight for a while. I stopped remembering the seven years in Q and started seeing ropes and gas pellets and electrodes attached to the shaved spots on the head. I wondered how they did it in Ontario. Different states have different ways. In Utah you can stand in front of a firing squad, if you want. And wave away the blindfold and look them in their eyes—

The best way to relax a muscle is to tighten it all the way and squeeze as hard as you can and then let it unwind completely. This, essentially, is what happened. By the time I'd cleared the cashier's check through our account I was functioning like a machine, gears meshing precisely, bearings oiled and motor in tune. By the time I was playing Hide-the-Gun on the plane for Chicago I was too preoccupied with doing things properly to worry about what might happen if I blew it. And with Chicago behind me and Omaha

coming up I could think about meeting Doug and col-
lecting the bank drafts and cashing them, and how
much money we would have and what my end would
be and whether or not it would be enough. I could
think about these things because I knew we were
clear. They were not going to tag us for this one.

Which led right into the part that was there all
along, hard to see but never hidden. We were making
out on this little deal. Everything had gone wrong, the
whole bundle had been snatched away when we were
already so close to it that we'd mentally spent it twice
over. Even so, we were making out. I was fifteen thousand dollars to the good no matter how you added it
up. All of that in a couple of months. Three, four years
of the salary they paid me at the Boulder Bowl.

So you figure it. I'd missed the girl and I'd missed
more than half of the money. The girl wouldn't bother
me long. I love them fast and hard with all the
dreamer's desperation, but once they're gone I don't
carry their ghosts around. I'd missed the girl and half of
the score, but fifteen thou was fifteen thou regardless.

There was a room waiting for me at the Mark Twain.
My name was Robert W. Pattison, and they had some
letters for me at the desk. I took them upstairs with
me. They were one of the batches of bank drafts, all
there and all in order, plus a note from Doug telling
me where I could find him. He'd left my suitcase with
the manager, and I called the desk and asked about it.
They apologized and sent a kid upstairs with it and he

went back downstairs half a dollar richer. I spent a long time under the shower tap, shaved close and clean, and put on fresh clothes. I picked the one suit I liked, a gray sharkskin with a double vent and patch pockets and just one button in the front. A suit John Hayden never wore in Olean.

I called Doug. He said he'd come around for me.

"I bought a car across the line in Kansas," he said. "I had to take a test and get a license and everything all over again. I thought it would come in handy."

"The car or the license?"

"Both of them."

I waited out front for him. The car was a Pontiac, two years old, long and low, a very dark green. It was the kind of car a very square businessman buys when he's feeling a little racy. I got in it and he drove while I talked. He seemed to know the city fairly well. It's bigger than it looks. He drove all over it while I talked.

He said, "You come out of this pretty good, don't you?"

"Do I?"

"Fifteen grand, isn't it? You didn't have a pot or a window a few months ago. Setting pins for a dime a line in Nothing, Colorado."

"Boulder," I said. "I didn't set pins. We had AMF automatic pin-spotters. I was the night man."

"Uh-huh."

"So you can just come out and say it, fellow."

He turned to face me and almost sideswiped a parked Ford. He cursed and I said something about him being lucky to pass the Kansas road test. You could feel it building up inside the car, like steam in a teakettle before it starts to whistle.

"I got a big hate on, Johnny."

"You've got company."

"You come off pretty. You can buy that craphouse in the mountains. Your end comes close enough to covering it. You were figuring loose and you know it. You come out fine."

"You've got the same fifteen I've got," I said easily. "On top of all you had to start with."

"But we missed the score, Johnny. And had to sweat at the end."

"Sweat never hurt."

"You let it go sour, Johnny."

"It started out sour. You crapped in the milk the first day out and now you wonder why it curdled. You got company with that hate, brother."

"Any time at all, Johnny."

"The money first."

It took us a couple of days. I had spread those bank drafts over four states, and we had to drive around and pick them up. It was nothing but mechanical but it had to be done. There was no rush to cash them. They were good any time, and in any place, and they had all been bought with cash. You could trace them to Canada, but you could not trace them to Parker or Whittlief or Rance or Hayden or Barnstable or Gunderman. They were all of them as good as government paper.

We drove around getting them from the post offices and hotels where I had sent them. We did not talk much. At night we took separate motel rooms and drank ourselves to sleep out of separate bottles. When we did talk, we generally got on each other's nerves. I was itching for him and he for me, but it had to wait and we were both of us good at waiting.

Then early one afternoon we picked up the last draft at a post office in a very little Iowa town. He asked me if that was the last one, and I told him it was. He stopped the car and we sliced the pie. We had cashed one of the drafts so that we could even things out properly. He took his expense money out, and the rest divided up into two even piles. My end was a little better than the estimated fifteen. About eight hundred better, plus assorted nickels and dimes.

And he said, "I'm ready when you are, Johnny."

"Now's a good time."

There was a motel coming up on the right. He nodded toward it. "Right here?"

"Cabins would be better."

"Uh-huh."

Three miles down the road there was one big shack and eighteen smaller ones. A sign advertised cabins for rent, three dollars for a double. There was one car in front of the office, another parked beside one of the cabins. Evidently they got the motel's overflow and the hot pillow trade and nothing more. Doug pulled off the road and I went into the office and rang for the manager.

He had the too-blue eyes of the alcoholic with a complementary sunburst of broken blood vessels at the bridge of his nose. I told him I wanted a cabin, the farthest one up on the north. He nodded and licked his thin lips.

I gave him three bucks. "We won't want to be disturbed," I said. "You hear any party noises from our cabin, anything at all, you just forget you heard a thing."

He winked at me. I let him dream his own dreams. Maybe he thought I had a fourteen year old girl in the car, maybe he figured I planned a spirited afternoon of rape. He did not mind.

I left the office and went back to the car. We drove over to the far cabin and parked. I opened the cabin door while Doug locked the car up tight. I nicked a light on. The cabin was stale and cheap. There was a bed, a bureau, and a chair. No rug on the floor. The mirror on the wall had a crack in it. I thought of a man or a woman waking up in a room like that one with a taste of whiskey and stale sex for morning company. A person could commit suicide in a cabin like that one.

Doug came in, closed the door, bolted it. "Whenever you're ready," he said, and I hit him in the face.

The punch didn't do much. He was backing up when I threw it and my fist glanced off the side of his face. He missed with a left and threw a right hand into my chest over the heart. I suddenly could not breathe. I ducked away from him and got hit a few times. I got my breath back, ducked under a punch and hit him in the pit of the stomach, hard. He doubled up and almost fell.

I went for him and kept missing. He spun away and ducked and dodged while I threw everything but the bed at him. He said, "Old man, I'm going to take you apart." I hit him again and he bounced back off a wall. I moved in low and he chopped me in the side of the head. A slew of colors danced inside my head. I felt myself slipping forward, put my hands out in front of me, caught his knee with the point of my chin. I snapped straight up and started over backward.

Everything was trying like hell to turn black. I wouldn't let go. He was standing over me, and I threw myself at his legs and held on. He tried to kick his way loose but didn't make it, and I got squared away and hauled his feet out from under him. He landed on top of me and threw a barrage of punches that bounced off my shoulders. I spun him around and tried to hit him but my arms wouldn't move all that well. I got up. He came up after me and shoved and I went over on to the bed. I kicked him coming in. The kick didn't have much power in it, but it caught him fairly square between the legs and put him on the floor again.

"You son of a bitch," he said.

He got up from the floor and I hauled myself off the bed and we stood in the middle of the room hitting each other. Neither of us had the energy to be cute. We had stopped dodging punches. We just kept hitting each other. I don't know if he felt the punches. I know I didn't, not any more.

I just stood there taking it and trying to beat the son of a bitch to the ground. I hit him and he hit me and I hit him and he hit me, over and over, just like that. We had screwed each other up but good, and we felt a clean uncomplicated hate for each other.

A heavy could have taken either of us. We were not strong-arm types. We were grifters, and grifters are rarely much help in a back-street brawl. He had some years on me, and maybe a couple of pounds, but we still wound up close to even.

Once his arms dropped and his eyes glazed over, and he stood there taking it while I hit him. He took a lot of punches before he went down. I stood over him, waiting, and he got up shaking his head and I swung and missed and he hit me square in the gut.

A little later he put another blow over the heart and I felt the way men must feel when they have a coronary. Everything froze, time and space, and I hung there breathless until he hit me in the face and put me down on the floor. I had trouble getting up. He asked me if I had had enough, and I pushed myself up and swung at him and missed, and he hit me again and I went down again. He didn't say anything this time. I got up and hit him, and hit him again, and we were back in the swing of things.

All of this seemed to go on forever. I spent more time on the floor than he did, but not too much more. It got so that it took less out of me to get hit than to lift an arm and throw a punch. We were both of us too arm-weary to do a hell of a lot of damage. And it ended finally with me tumbling back against a wall and holding onto it and sliding down it toward the floor while he sagged backward and sat down on the bed and then lay backward, half on the bed and half on the floor. Neither one of us moved after that, not for a long time.

There was no john in the cabin, just a sink. He washed up, went out to the car to get us some fresh clothes. We took our time cleaning up and changing. We were both of us pretty bloody. He had a split lip, a few cuts on his face, swellings under both eyes. I wasn't cut up quite that much but I had managed to lose one tooth somewhere along the line and my jaw was in fairly sad shape.

Doug was the first to talk. He was looking in the mirror, and he shook his head and said, "Beautiful."

"We're both pretty."

"You can sure as hell take a few punches, Johnny."

"I should have been a boxer."

"Yeah. Both of us. I can't find my cigarettes."

I dug out a pair of mine and gave him one. We chucked our dirty clothes in the corner and went out to the car. He headed north, drove slowly.

"It was a good idea, stopping here," he said after a while. "I was aching for a crack at you ever since Toronto."

"Well, we worked it out."

"We did at that," he said.

I smoked my cigarette all the way down and flipped

the butt out the window. I asked him what he figured on doing next.

"I suppose I'll head for Vegas," he said.

"To give the money back across the tables?"

"Part of it. Or I'll beat them for a change. I like it out there. Get some sun, lie around the pool, get a little drunk, rest up while I figure out how to connect for the next one."

"Sure."

"I guess I'll drive. I lucked out on the car, bought the first one off the lot and it doesn't ride bad at all. I figure I can drive it to Vegas with no trouble."

"You'll want a new name."

"Well, that's no headache, Johnny. Pick a new name and sell it to myself and then register it in Nevada with Nevada plates. I'll probably put it in my own name, I don't know. Maybe not." He was silent a moment. "I have to pass through Colorado, I guess. Or close enough to it. If you feel like riding along, feel free."

I didn't answer him right away. I thought about a lot of things, added them up and checked the addition.

"Maybe I'll ride on through with you," I said. "I could use a vacation. I don't even remember what Vegas looks like."

He looked at me.

"I don't gamble much," I went on. "But the sunshine sounds good, and all the rest."

"I figured you were anxious to get back to your town."

"Well," I said.

"And you'll be tight enough on money. You wouldn't want to blow some of it in Vegas. Even without gambling—"

I lit another cigarette. I thought that it was funny how a couple of days took the prison fever right out of a man. Running the risks and being utterly in tune and getting everything right and beating the system did wonders for you. Lost confidence came back. You found out, once again, just who you happened to be.

"I'll just take things easy in Vegas," I said finally. The words came easy now. "And we'll both of us keep our eyes open, you and I, and when the right proposition comes along we'll be ready for it. Next time we'll play it straight. We've got enough troubles without conning each other."

"You—" He stopped, started over. "You want to work with me again?"

"Why not? We're a good match for each other. We work damned well together. We already proved that much."

"But—"

"We both made mistakes we won't make again. They don't change the fact that we make a good team."

He drove a mile or two in silence. "That roadhouse in Colorado," he said.

"What about it?"

"You figure you need one more score to afford it?"

It would have been easy to say yes, sure, that was it. But it wasn't, and I was not about to say so. So I thought for a minute or two, and I pictured myself standing behind a bar wiping glasses, or sitting in an office keeping careful records for the tax beagles, or figuring interest rates and depreciation schedules and breakage allowances. I thought about the last few days and I thought too about the weeks before them. The tension, the feeling of running wide open with the gears meshing and all the machinery perfectly aligned. I thought about The Dream, and I thought about The Girl, and about all dreams and all girls. No dreams come true, I guess, and no girls are as perfect as the heart would have them.

And beyond all that, I thought that a man must be what he is and do what he is geared to do. He cannot permit himself to be conned out of what he truly is. Not by the scare of a prison cell. Not by the smell of a woman, or the teasing song of a dream.

So I told Doug this, or most of it, and maybe he understood, and maybe he did not. At least I did. He pulled out to pass another car and put the gas pedal down on the floor. The sun was about gone but we were heading toward where it had disappeared from sight. West, toward Las Vegas.

Get Hard Case Crime by Mail...
And Save 43%!

☐ **YES! Sign me up for the Hard Case Crime Book Club!**

As long as I choose to stay in the club, I will receive every Hard Case Crime book as it is published (generally one each month). I'll get to preview each title for 10 days. If I decide to keep it, I will pay only $3.99* — a savings of 43% off the cover price! There is no minimum number of books I must buy and I may cancel my membership at any time.

Name: _____

Address: _____

City / State / ZIP: _____

Telephone: _____

E-Mail: _____

☐ **I want to pay by credit card:** ☐ VISA ☐ MasterCard ☐ Discover

Card #: _____ Exp. date: _____

Signature: _____

Mail this page to:

HARD CASE CRIME BOOK CLUB
20 Academy Street, Norwalk, CT 06850-4032

Or fax it to 610-995-9274.
You can also sign up online at www.dorchesterpub.com.

* Plus $2.00 for shipping. Offer open to residents of the U.S. and Canada only. Canadian residents please call 1-800-481-9191 for pricing information.

If you are under 18, a parent or guardian must sign. Terms, prices, and conditions subject to change. Subscription subject to acceptance. Dorchester Publishing reserves the right to reject any order or cancel any subscription.